HIGH DESERT
GRAVE ROBBER

HIGH DESERT
GRAVE ROBBER

LINDA A. MORTON

Interior design and formatting by:

E.M.
TIPPETTS
BOOK DESIGNS

www.emtippettsbookdesigns.com

CHAPTER 1

May 15, 1987

The parking lot would be full this Friday afternoon as tourists began to flock to this high desert art community of Santa Fe, New Mexico. Amongst other vehicles, the yellow VW Bug would stand out. The blue Honda Civic was searching for a parking spot. It stopped two spaces away from the yellow car. Time to act.

The eighty-three-degree temperature today caused tire pressures to increase so the blade would seep through the rubber easily. First, open the switchblade and look around. Then, dip down to stab the back tire and withdraw the knife quickly. The tire deflated as hot air seeped out.

Onto the other side. First, a look around. Someone is

approaching and sounds like men talking. Close the blade and slip it in the back pocket. Start walking away, then return when the nearby car leaves. Safe for now. Return to the yellow car.

Open the blade, dip down and stab the rubber. Done!

Having returned to the blue Honda, the knife was tucked into the console. Next to it was a brown vial of powder. The vial was put into the lunch bag for use later. It was time to get back to work.

The blue Honda parked in its usual spot. The knife was returned. In a few hours, the rest of the plan would be set into motion. The driver of the yellow Bug would come back and would be in need of a ride home. She would be offered a cold soda with a dab of white powder mixed in. They would drive around town until the passenger passed out.

Wait until dark, then unload the passenger.

By nine p.m., the blue sedan found a secluded grassy area off the main road and turned off the lights. No one was in sight. It was a struggle pulling the limp body out of the passenger seat as it fell to the ground. Something caught on the seat, then fell to the floor. The sound of metal. No time to look for it. Grab under the arms and drag the body away from the road. Hide it in the tall grass. Get back to the car and head out. All went as planned and home by nine forty-five.

THE SANTA FE JOURNAL

Monday, May 18, 1987

A body was found on the campus of the College of Santa Fe early Sunday evening. Hikers discovered the body lying in an area of tall grass. Police confirmed that it was a female student who attended the IAIA. The coroner stated the body had been dead up to forty-eight hours. Cause of death is unknown at this time. The name is not being released until the next of kin is notified. If you or someone you know has any information, please contact the Santa Fe Police Department.

The college dorm was filled with female students preparing to get to their classes when word got out about the body found off the side of the road last night. On each floor, women huddled together in fear as they wondered who the female student was. They thought they were safe here, but not anymore.

Part of the allure of this campus were the wide-open spaces with vistas of the mountain range. As the small groups dispersed to leave for their classes, they were met on the first floor by police officers.

One by one, the students were asked for their names and

whereabouts over the weekend. Officers took each student aside for questioning. "Did you see anyone suspicious on campus recently? Has anyone told you they had been threatened or had reason to be afraid? Did someone in the Dormitory have enemies they mentioned to you? Did you notice if anyone in the Dorm was acting unusual lately? Did you hear anyone arguing recently?" So far, no one had any information.

On the dorm's third floor, Marie had taken a shower and was playing music louder than usual since her roommate wasn't home. It was nice to have the place to herself a couple of days, though it was odd that Joyce didn't let her know she'd be gone. Marie looked out the window to a clear blue sky, then noticed a squad car in front of the building. Class started in thirty minutes, so time to go. As she descended to the first floor, she was stopped by an officer.

"Miss, we're questioning everyone in the women's dorm because the body of a female student was found nearby last night. Your name?" The officer asked.

"That's horrible! My name is Marie Ferris." Marie started shaking in the knees as fear set in. "Who is it? Do you know?"

"We're not releasing the identity until the family is notified. Did you notice anything suspicious around campus recently? Do you know someone who has been threatened?" The officer observed Marie lean on the counter for support. Marie's heart was racing.

Her eyes widened as Marie cupped her hands over her face. "I don't know about that, but something is unusual, officer. My roommate didn't come home over the weekend. She usually tells me if she won't be home. She went to work after class on Friday and hasn't returned. I hope she's all right, but now I'm worried."

The officer escorted Marie to a corner table and chairs where she could sit, away from the other students. "Tell me about your roommate, Marie." The officer had pen and paper ready to write.

"Her name is Joyce. Joyce Two Feathers Jordan. She's Cherokee. She came from her home in Oklahoma to Santa Fe to study sculpture here at IAIA. She's so sweet." Marie got teary-eyed. She paused to take a deep breath before she continued. "She was so happy to be here. She had a part-time job in town at an art gallery."

"What's the name of the gallery, Marie?" The officer asked.

"Canon, the J. D. Canon Gallery. There's an area in town called Gallery Row. I don't know the address. She's been working there a few months now."

"How did she get there? Did she drive or take a bus? Did she say anything to you recently that might have been cause for concern?" the officer asked.

"She had her car, a yellow VW Bug. She didn't say much about work, but she did seem concerned about something recently. She didn't talk about it." Marie responded. Tears began to fall as she asked "Oh, officer, was it Joyce's body that was found out there?"

"We can't confirm the identity at this time. The school will let you know." The officer thanked Marie and got on the radio to his Chief.

CHAPTER 2

May 21

It was Thursday and second grade teacher, Laura Barnes, was almost finished entering her students' final grades. School ended in May here in the high desert since many classrooms had no air conditioning and it got very hot.

The principal popped in. "Laura, are you ready for the last day of school?" asked Mrs. Lopez.

"Just about. All grades will be entered and report cards ready to go home tomorrow." Laura responded.

"Do you have any plans for summer break? If not, you can always teach summer school." Mrs. Lopez had asked the staff last month and Laura didn't respond.

"Actually, I'm interviewing for a job Friday at an art gallery in town. I was an Art Major before I studied to become a teacher, you know." Laura explained.

"Yes, I noticed that on your resume when you applied to work here. I like that you have other interests to bring to your teaching career. I'll see you at Friday's Assembly, Laura."

"Yes. I'll see you there, Mrs. Lopez." Laura turned off the computer. *One more day to go.*

As Laura walked to her car in the hot sun, beads of sweat were forming on her forehead. "I am so ready to finish this school year" she muttered to herself. As she settled into her hot car, Laura turned on the radio to her favorite jazz station and turned on the air conditioner. *Time to relax.*

She had a taste for a green chili cheeseburger. She drove down St. Francis Drive to her favorite drive-through burger restaurant and ordered her usual. She had grown fond of green chile on almost everything since she had moved here from the Midwest. She sat in her cooled car while savoring the flavors of the Southwest.

On her way home to her casita, she observed how the yellow Chamisa flowers were covering the hills. There were a few heavy snowfalls this past winter, she recalled. Laura opened her window. Now sage and lavender scented the mountain air. She took in a deep breath while her curly brown hair swirled around her face.

Laura took Old Pecos Trail into town, then merged with Old Santa Fe Trail. The state Capitol was in view now. While stopped at a red light, she noticed some sort of protest had gathered on the Capitol grounds. Legislators and staff came and went through the large brass doors where Security officers stood guard.

She closed her window so as not to take in nearby car fumes. The light changed. Laura turned right on Paseo de Peralta and took Acequia Madre home.

She took her dogs for a walk, then settled in for the night. Laura prepared for two events the next day: Her last day of the school year and her job interview at the J.D. Canon Gallery. She laid out two sets of clothes, set the alarm clock and fell fast asleep.

By mid-morning Friday, the Awards Assembly was over and people dispersed through-out the school. Proud parents who were gathered in the tiered bleachers earlier now exited to the front entrance of the school. Students went back to classrooms with their teachers. Laura handed out report cards and gave each student a book to read over the summer. "Don't stop reading just because you're on break." she told her students.

One by one, students came to Laura's desk and brought gifts. She received flowers, coffee mugs, boxes of chocolate, drawings and ornaments that said "Best Teacher Ever."

"Oh, thank you. How kind of you. That's so sweet." she said as the students approached.

The first dismissal bell rang and students packed up to

leave for the buses. Five minutes later, the second bell rang. Time for kids to meet the parents outside. "Bye! Have a great summer!" Laura yelled out.

When the classroom emptied, Laura packed up her gifts in a box, turned off the lights and closed the door. She visited some teachers whose students didn't often give gifts and handed them a surprise from her box of presents. "I'll see you in August!" Laura said with excitement. As protocol required, she turned in her room keys to the school secretary at the front office.

Laura walked briskly to her car and thought of her interview in two hours.

It was just a half-day of school so she got home early. Salad was a good choice for lunch, since her nerves were getting jittery. Laura took her dogs for a short walk, fed the cat and changed clothes for her interview. She felt refreshed.

Laura checked her purse for ID, keys and pepper spray. Since being newly single, she always took the spray when she went walking. After five blocks, Laura's nerves had calmed. She entered the J.D. Canon Gallery with anticipation.

A tall thin woman with straight blonde hair saw her enter. "Can I help you?" she asked.

"Yes. My name is Laura Barnes. I'm here for an interview for the summer position."

"Oh, yes. Follow me." They walked up a few stairs to an office. "Take a seat. I'm the Manager, Anita Boles."

"Nice to meet you, Ms. Boles." Laura replied.

"Now, I'll tell you what we need and you tell me why you think you are qualified." Anita started. "We need someone who is punctual and neatly dressed, no blue jeans or sandals. Someone who is friendly to visitors and observant. Staff is expected to stand in their areas and make sure no one steals anything or damages the art. There is a forty-five-minute lunch and there are two fifteen minute breaks. Can you stand for long periods of time, Laura? Sitting is not allowed unless on break."

"Well, I walk a lot so I believe I can do that. Does the gallery have a sales quota for summer and part-time staff?" Laura inquired.

"It would be great if you sold art, but there's no quota for part-timers. You would be here mainly to protect the artwork and to greet the visitors. Since you're a teacher, I know you would have passed a background check. If you did happen to make a sale, you would let me know. I write up the sales. Tell me, why do you want to work here, Laura?"

"I studied art in college and want to do something different on my summer break." Laura replied. "Plus, I live nearby, so this is a convenient location."

Just then, the office door opened and in walked a white-haired man wearing blue jeans and a plaid short-sleeved shirt. Laura noticed his penny loafers had dust on them. He was wearing white socks that were dusty, too. His ruddy complexion indicated he spent a lot of time in the sun and burned easily. She wondered if he was the grounds keeper or gardener.

"So, Anita, who do we have here?" he asked as he eyed Laura top to bottom. "Mr. Canon, this is Laura Barnes, an applicant for the summer position."

He held out a clammy hand and Laura shook it. She discreetly wiped her hand on her skirt. "You're the school teacher, right?" Laura smiled and nodded yes. "Welcome aboard, Laura. Why don't you start on Monday since Saturdays can get busy. We'll start you out slow. Be here at 9 a.m. sharp."

"Yes, sir. I'll be here. Thank you." Laura looked at Anita. "I guess I'm hired."

"Yes. It seems so. Just be sure you follow the rules." Anita said as she escorted Laura out of the gallery.

When Laura got home, she called her mother. "Mom, I'm finished with school for the year and I'm starting a summer job on Monday. I'll be working at the J.D. Canon Gallery on the famous Gallery Row. I'm so excited!"

"Well, that sounds interesting. I know you always liked art. Is it far from your casita ?" her mom asked.

"No, it's about five blocks away. I can walk there. I met the owner, Mr. Canon. He's nothing like I thought he'd be. He's very plain looking. I thought he was the gardener, at first. I had heard there was a lovely garden in the back."

"Well, Laura, it's been quite a year for you, getting divorced while working full time. You had to leave your large home and find a new place on your own. I hope you can afford to live there."

"I'll be fine, mom. I'll work as much as I need to. It's better than staying in a miserable marriage. If I have to work part-time during the school year, I will. For now, I'll work five days a week for eight weeks at the gallery. I'll save money by walking instead of driving to work and I can bring sack lunches instead of eating out. I'll let you know how it goes. Say hi to dad for me." Laura hung up the phone and prepared dinner.

Blue corn enchiladas with green chile was savored while watching the news on the local TV station. Laura saw a picture of a young woman with long black hair. She turned up the volume.

"The body of a female art student found on the campus of the College of Santa Fe Sunday has been identified as that of Joyce Two Feathers Jordan of the Cherokee Nation. She was a student at IAIA. Details have not been released about the cause of death. There are no suspects in custody. If you have information about this case., contact the Santa Fe Police Department."

Laura was saddened at the news of this young woman's fate. She hadn't watched much local news lately. Laura decided to be more alert and observant of her surroundings.

She thought Santa Fe was a quiet art community and took safety for granted. She needed to be more careful.

She got the dogs on their leashes and head out for their evening walk. The streets were quiet and few cars drove by. Laura heard the trickle of water running in the acequia as she strolled the narrow sidewalks of Acequia Madre. The dogs tugged on their leashes and Laura restrained them from walking in the muddy water. The sun was setting and the mountain air cooled. Though it was hot during the day, the nights were cool enough for a light jacket. Laura shivered in her Tee shirt and head back home.

Laura planned her weekend: Go shopping for some new outfits, get groceries for the week, clean the casita and exercise the dogs. Visit the Fine Arts Museum on Sunday. Look for a book on the early artists of Santa Fe and Taos. She wanted to be ready for the first day of her new job.

CHAPTER 3

May 25

Monday came fast and Laura arrived at the gallery at nine. She was shown by another staffer, Carol, where to clock in and where the restroom and lounge were. Laura learned that Carol had worked here for five years. The two women made their way through each room of the gallery and then to the garden. Laura asked if she could eat her lunch in the garden and Carol said it would be fine unless there was a private party or other event going on.

Carol added "A few words of advice: Don't ask too many questions of Mr. Canon, he doesn't like it. His family lives on-site temporarily and his daughter is a friend of Anita's. The family visits the gallery and they will want to meet you.

There's a young man in shipping, Tom, who does odd jobs around the gallery. He wears a baseball cap. You may see him around. Mr. Canon has an eye for the young ladies, so be advised. Anita makes the rules and she's a hawk. Don't cross her."

"What do you mean, she's a hawk?" Laura asked.

"She watches everything and everyone. She's very protective of the Canon family. We had a nice young lady work here. She saw Mr. Canon's private collection in his office and I heard her ask him where he got his items. Before I knew it, she was gone. Anita said she was fired. That was just last week, Friday. I guess you're her replacement." Carol explained.

"I guess I am. I'm just here for the summer." Laura said.

"Well, a lot can happen over the summer. Let's get back inside."

When they returned, Anita was looking for the two women. "Laura, you'll work in the textile room this week. Make sure the rugs are kept neatly folded. There's a book for reference you can read until visitors come in. Meet and greet and no sitting, remember? I'll let you know when you can take a break."

"Yes, I understand." Laura felt like saying *Aye, aye, Sir,* but refrained.

"Carol, you will go between the Santa Fe Art Colony and the Taos Founders rooms. I will be in the front of the gallery in my office where I can hear visitors as they arrive. If I see a regular collector, I will personally assist them. Mr. Canon will be here shortly. Any questions, Laura?"

"No, Ms. Boles. I'll let you know if I do."

The gallery had a steady stream of tourists and locals who enjoyed viewing the works of the Santa Fe Art Colony, Taos Founders, contemporary Native American sculpture and great western painters. Some art sold for tens of thousands of dollars.

American Indian rugs of all designs were on display in the area Laura was assigned to. She had read about southwestern textiles in college at UNM. Laura knew the Two Grey Hills weavers used only natural-colored wool. She looked at the sales tags on the rugs for more information. After an hour and a half, Anita came to say Laura could take a break. Great!

She went to the lounge, where she got a granola bar and cup of coffee. It was nice to sit down for a few minutes. She heard a discussion outside of the lounge with the sound of a radio, a police radio. Laura finished her snack and opened the door to see a police officer outside of Anita's office. The officer motioned to Laura to wait there.

The officer asked Anita "Did Joyce Two Feathers Jordan work here? When did you see her last? Did you notice if she was troubled by something?"

"Yes, she worked here for a few months. Nice girl. I had to fire her for not meeting her sales quota. She didn't like losing her job, but those are the rules. Her last day was Friday, May 15. I haven't seen her since." Anita responded. "Is there anything else? I need to get back to work."

The officer gave Anita his card, then approached Laura. "What is your name? Did you know Joyce Jordan?"

"My name is Laura Barnes. I just started working here today, officer. I didn't know Joyce. I'm sorry to hear about her death. I heard her name on the news last night and that she was found on the college campus."

"Yes, that's correct. As far as we know, the gallery is the last place she was seen. If you think of anything, call this number." He gave her his card. The officer then proceeded to go to Mr. Canon's office.

On the way back to the textile room, Laura noticed the owner's office door was open. She briefly observed what Carol described as the private collection. She heard the officer and Mr. Canon talking. "She was a sweet girl." Canon said. "I'm sorry to hear this. Last I saw her was Friday, May 15, I think it was."

Laura saw Carol and said "An officer is interviewing everyone about Joyce Jordan, the woman whose body was found last week. He said she worked here. Did you know her?" Laura asked.

"Yes, poor girl. She was an American Indian studying sculpture at IAIA. She enjoyed working here. I really liked

Joyce. It's horrible that she died." Carol's expression showed a real sadness.

"Carol, the officer said the gallery was the last place Joyce was seen alive."

Anita approached the women now. "OK, ladies, get back to work. I don't want you discussing this issue about Joyce with anyone, do you understand?"

"Yes, Ms. Boles." Laura responded and left the room. The officer approached Carol now and Anita stayed on to observe.

"Yes, officer, I knew Joyce. She worked here part-time. I saw her Friday, May 15. I didn't see her the following Saturday, a day she usually worked. When I asked where she was, I was told she was fired." Carol looked at Anita, and Anita shook her head in agreement. Carol was reluctant to say anything more since Anita was monitoring the conversation. The officer gave Carol his card and proceeded to the shipping area to interview more staff.

Only a few visitors came through to look around the textile room before it was time for lunch. Laura got her sack lunch and went to the garden. Sculptures were standing between bushes and around the flowers. They looked real. She found a bench in a shady spot. It was a warm and sunny day and the sky was a clear blue.

She reflected on her past year, getting divorced and resettling on her own. She didn't get much out of the divorce settlement, only enough to buy a new car and put a security deposit down on a casita nearby. Though Laura didn't have her vegetable garden and passive solar home in Eldorado, she had a charming place where she could keep her dogs and cat. She had what she needed.

She was just finishing her sandwich when Mr. Canon approached her. She still had a few minutes left on her break and wondered what was on his mind. "Hey, Laura, do you want to see something really special? I just brought it in today."

"Sure, Mr. Canon."

"Oh, just call me J.D." he replied in kind of a southern drawl. She followed him to a large room off the garden. Carol had said that Mr. Canon was building a house in town and lived on the gallery premises for the time being with his wife and children.

Laura was feeling cautious since she was warned that Mr. Canon put on the charm with younger female employees. She hoped he was not going to put her in an embarrassing situation. He smelled of old-time cologne and sweat. She tried to keep her distance from him.

Laura followed the owner to the pool table in the middle of the room. She observed floor-to-ceiling shelves filled with books and large ceramics. The room was dimly lit, though outside was bright and sunny. She felt uncomfortable being alone with the man.

She saw something on the pool table, lying on a white sheet. She squinted. They were bones. Human bones! They filled the length of the pool table and had dirt on them. Laura gasped in horror!

J.D. Canon grinned and said proudly "Isn't it amazing?"

"Who is this?" Laura was starting to feel dizzy from the musty smell of dirt on the human remains.

"It looks like an entire male skeleton. I believe it's a Native American, probably early Pueblo. I found a few things next to it, too." He boasted.

"I've never seen anything like it. How did you get this?" Laura tried to make conversation, but did not like what she saw. Her heart was beating rapidly and blood was rushing to her face.

"Oh, I have land outside of town where I do some digging. I found it under some stones." He replied.

Laura felt sick to her stomach and said "I have to go, Mr. Canon. I'll be late." The gallery owner laughed "OK, Laura. Go back to work."

She turned, searched for the door and head to the employee restroom inside. Lunch was backing up in her throat and she was gagging. She got to the sink just in time to heave. Her face was red and puffy now. Laura filled her hands with cold water and splashed her face a few times. She cupped her hands to gather some water to drink, then spit it out. She took deep breaths and wiped her face dry. A cough drop helped soothe her throat. She had to get back to work.

Carol looked at Laura sternly and said "Anita is looking for you."

In the textile room, a German couple was asking Anita for assistance. "Yes, I'll get someone to help you, just a minute." Anita assured them. She turned sharply, agitated that Laura wasn't back in her station.

Just then, Laura entered and forced a smile to greet the visitors. She averted Anita's glare and pursed lips. "Hello. What can I help you with?"

"Guten tag, fraulein. This rug here. We like the design. Can you tell us about it?" They asked in a thick German accent.

Laura replied. "Oh, I love your accent! This rug was woven in the area of Two Grey Hills in northwestern New Mexico. The weavers there use only the wool from the colors of their flock: brown, grey, black and ivory. This Navajo weaver won a top award at last year's Indian Market. It's a juried show with a lot of competition." Laura looked at the tag more closely. "This rug measures six by nine feet and is priced at $9000.00."

The couple was enthralled and the husband said "Das gut!" They wanted the textile.

Laura had her first sale. "Can I help you find anything else?" she asked.

"Nein." They responded. "We are happy to take this home to Germany with us."

Laura carried the textile and escorted them to the front office. "Anita will write up a receipt and have it packed for you."

"Danke, fraulein. Thank you, miss." The couple proceeded with their transaction.

Laura felt better. She returned to her station and greeted new visitors. Thirty minutes later, Anita came over. "I have to ask why you were late from lunch. When one person is late, it sets other schedules off."

Laura's smile faded. "I had an upset stomach after eating and I stayed in the restroom until I felt better. I'm sorry." Laura didn't want to explain what caused her to feel sick.

"If it happens again, I'll have to dock your pay. Follow the rules, Laura. Oh, yes, congratulations on your sale." Anita said coldly and left the room.

Laura didn't like Anita's sarcastic tone of voice. It was just her first day on the job and she'd already been interviewed by the police and saw human remains.

So far, the gallery world was more adventurous than she expected.

The next few days were uneventful. She read about textiles and artists of Santa Fe and Taos. Mr. Canon had not approached her since Monday.

On Friday, Laura observed that Anita and Mr. Canon seemed very nervous, even pacing the floor. A man with a pony tail, an American Indian, went room to room without talking to anyone. When he came by the owner's office, he looked in. His eyes roamed the ceiling and walls. Mr. Canon politely closed the door, telling the man that he had a meeting inside. Anita approached and asked if she could help the visitor.

"I'm interested in seeing the items in this room." The man said.

Anita responded. "It's a private collection of the owner's and not for sale, sir."

"I'd like to know where those items came from." the man stated.

"I can't tell you where they came from, but Mr. Canon has an excellent reputation as an art dealer." The manager knew that most of the collection had no receipts, but she never asked how her boss attained them. She didn't want anyone else questioning him either. "Can I get your name and contact information so the owner can call you?"

"I'll come back." The man left with clenched fists.

Once inside his car, the professor lit a sage stick and purified himself with the smoke. He returned to Albuquerque, where he would discuss what he saw with the Elders.

Inside, Anita breathed a sigh of relief. She told Laura to take her lunch break. Then, Anita visited the owner in his office. "The man didn't leave his contact information, so we can't locate him. He asked about your collection and said he'll come back."

"Yes, this can be a problem." Canon replied in a worried tone.

Just then, his wife and daughter entered. "We're going out for lunch, dad. Do you want to join us? You look like you could use a change of scenery."

"Yes, that's a great idea! Let's go to the Purple Adobe." The three family members left the gallery.

Laura observed Anita in the owner's office looking closely at items on the wall. She noticed Laura and said "If anyone asks, these items are not for sale. It's a private collection and you know nothing about them. Understood?"

CHAPTER 4

May 30

Over the Memorial Day weekend, Laura took long morning walks with her dogs along the streets of Santa Fe's eastside neighborhood. Large adobe homes sat behind iron gates. Many of the larger homes had casitas in the back. Laura learned these casitas started as residences for extended family. If not used by family, they were rented out.

The afternoon was hot. Laura had lunch then took a short siesta. There were festivities on the Plaza this Sunday afternoon. A vintage car show was of interest, so Laura walked downtown. She enjoyed looking at the old and the new model cars. They were all nicely detailed and polished.

Some car owners talked to visitors while others cruised slowly around the side streets. Some of the cars were Low Riders, which were famous around parts of New Mexico.

The vendors were out selling tamales, Frito Pie, ice cream and drinks. Laura got a strawberry milkshake and strolled past the Palace of the Governors, where the American Indian artists displayed their handmade items. There were so many beautiful things to look at. Laura decided to come back another time to get something for her mother. She picked up a copy of The Albuquerque Times and head home.

She pulled out her lawn chair, brought the dogs out and read the paper in the warm afternoon sun. Since Laura was a graduate of UNM, she liked to read news about the university. Today, there was an article by a UNM professor, Dr. John Buffalo. He looked somewhat familiar. She began reading.

It's time that Tribal Nations get their burial items returned. Across the southwest, you can find galleries that display artifacts that could have only come from the graves of Indigenous people. For many years, looting of graves has persisted and a market to sell burial items has flourished. There have to be more laws enacted and enforced to prevent desecration of our tribal lands.

Laura knew why this man looked familiar. He was in the gallery on Friday.

May 31

Though this Monday was a holiday, the gallery was open. There were lots of visitors in town and the gallery took advantage of that. Laura felt rested for another week at the gallery. She was still working in the textile room today.

People came and went. A tall man with blonde hair was looking at the rugs now. Laura approached and asked if she could help him with something. He turned and smiled at her.

"No, I'm just looking, thank you." Laura moved aside and observed the man. He was wearing dark jeans, cowboy boots, a white dress shirt, a Bolo tie and beige corduroy jacket. She knew this was professional men's attire here, in Santa Fe. Not the two-piece suit and tie worn in the Midwest, where Laura grew up. This was a mix of casual and refined. When he turned around, she noticed a silver buckle and belt tip, a Ranger Set. They were made by silversmiths and sold in fine shops around the Plaza. *Expensive.*

As Laura was observing him, the tall man found her eyes and asked "You could help me with something. Where's a good place for lunch nearby? I'm up from Albuquerque and don't know the area."

"Well, if you're walking, cross the Santa Fe River bridge and go left on Alameda Street. Walk towards town to Old Santa Fe Trail. If you go left towards the Capitol Building, you'll see the Purple Adobe Restaurant and Bar. They have green chili stew and great southwestern meatloaf. The owner is a painter so her art is displayed. If you go right at the Trail, there's La Fonda Hotel with a pastry shop and a restaurant. There's even a diner in the drugstore on the Plaza that's famous for its Frito Pie. I hope this helps."

"Yes, they all sound good. I'll go to the Purple Adobe. My car is in the lot nearby, so that's perfect. Thank you, miss."

Laura smiled and said "You're very welcome, sir. Come again."

Laura found the man to be of interest, attractive. She liked his smile and his cologne was slightly intoxicating. She hoped he would return.

She watched him leave and noticed he stopped outside the owner's office. He looked around the room slowly. A staff member approached and he nodded his head in acknowledgement before exiting the gallery.

Laura became alerted to the fact that a group of teenagers came into the Textile Room. They were giggling and chatting. "Can I help you with something?"

A brown-haired girl with a pierced nose said "We're on an assignment from our art teacher. We have to visit a gallery and find a work of art that we can write about. We saw paintings, sculpture, jewelry, now the rugs."

"Well, I can show you a few rugs," said Laura. "Some of these textiles are hung on the wall or framed. Some are used on the floor. Some have natural-colored wool, like this Two

Grey Hills rug. Some have vegetable dyes. The designs have meaning. For instance, this is a Storm pattern with lightning designs. This is a Sand Painting which has a connection to healing ceremonies for Navajo Indians. This is a Yei pattern. In Navajo mythology, the Yei are supernatural beings."

Laura continued. "If the weaver has won awards, the price is higher. The weavers are Navajo Indian from New Mexico and Arizona. If you want more information to write about these textiles, there are books for sale in the front of the gallery. You can, also, go to the public library."

As Laura spoke and displayed the textiles, the students drew sketches of patterns they liked. "We have enough for our assignment now. Some of these designs are really cool. Thank you, Miss." The girls discussed which designs they liked best as they left the room.

Laura enjoyed talking to the young people. It reminded her that she was still a teacher.

CHAPTER 5

June 3

As Laura approached the gallery entrance, she saw a man and two Elders enter the gallery. She recognized the younger man as the professor who was quoted in the Albuquerque Times recently. She clocked in and greeted the men waiting in the main room. The Elders has striped blankets over their shoulders.

Anita approached them and the professor said "We are here to see Mr. Canon about his artifact collection."

The manager recalled this was the same man who came earlier. "I don't know when you can see him, but please take a seat. I'm the manager, Anita Boles, and you are?"

"My name is Professor John Buffalo. These men are Pueblo Elders Reese and Mirabal."

The men waited quietly and Anita told Laura to work in the adjacent room, the Santa Fe Art Colony Collection. Laura browsed the room and kept an eye and ear open for what may transpire in the main room. The men looked very serious, even mad. They didn't look like customers or tourists. Why were they here?

Laura looked at the paintings and names of the artists whose works were displayed in the room. She had heard of Will Shuster and Gustave Baumann. They were the co-creators of the famous Zozobra. She found a binder provided by the gallery for a quick reference to biographies of early New Mexico artists. She scanned the pages for highlights of the artists' lives.

Laura heard men's voices and stood near the adjacent room. Mr. Canon was overheard saying "Mr. Buffalo, I don't know why you want to see my artifacts. They are my personal collection and are not for sale."

"These men are Elders from the Pueblo Council, Mr. Reese and Mr. Mirabal. We came to see your collection because we think you have sacred items that belong to the Pueblo people and other Tribal Nations. I saw some of these items during a recent visit when your office door was open. It now seems it's open for visitors, other than Indigenous people." The professor stated.

"Sometimes my office door is open, but not always. I will open the door for viewing from the doorway only." replied Canon reluctantly.

Anita stood nearby anxiously, knowing Mr. Canon did not want to do this.

The men approached the door and the Elders gasped when they looked in. The younger professor braced their elbows as they looked around the walls.

Elder Reese pointed and said. "There's a Sun Dance Shield from the Dakota Tribes and fans of eagle feathers. How did you acquire them?"

"I don't recall." Replied Canon.

Mr. Mirabal pointed to the ceiling. "That's a Blackfoot Thunder Pipe used for prayers by Montana's Blackfeet Tribes. There are many Spirit Masks. Where did you get these, Mr. Canon?"

"Different parts of the American west that I've explored over the years. I can't be specific. It was open land." The gallery owner replied, getting annoyed by the questioning.

"That's a Shaman's Neck Ring on that wall" the professor said pointing to the object. He saw bear claws, cedar bark and fur. "Do you know where it came from, Mr. Canon?"

"I don't recall. Gentlemen, I'll have to ask you to leave. I have an appointment."

The three men scanned the room and saw many more

burial items. They lowered their heads. Their suspicions were confirmed.

"Thank you, Mr. Canon, for allowing us to see your collection. We will go now." John Buffalo said as he took the arms of the two Elders and turned to leave. He escorted them outside.

Canon let out a long sigh when the men left. He had a bad feeling about the visit. Anita caught his eye and shook her head, knowing trouble was brewing.

Before entering their vehicle, Elder Reese said "Wait." He reached in his coat pocket and took out a stick of dried sage leaves and a lighter. He lit the smudge stick and waved the smoke toward his face and body, then handed it to Elder Mirabal for the cleansing ritual. John Buffalo then cleansed himself spiritually and crushed the burning sage tip in the gravel.

Once in the car, John opened his window and looked out. "We will talk to the Pueblo Council about our next steps. Many of those items were buried with the Shaman and Warriors who used them. The only way they could be found is to dig up the graves. We have a high desert grave robber here in Santa Fe." The scent of sage lingered in the air. The men were solemn on their long ride home.

Upon their return to the Albuquerque area, Elder Reese sent messages to members of the Pueblo Council and other

Tribal Nations. "Upon visiting the J.D. Canon Gallery in Santa Fe, we believe many of the artifacts in the owner's collection are stolen from graves of our ancestors. Displayed there are burial items that could have only been dug up. We must demand the return of our sacred items. A show of unity is necessary."

A meeting of the Council was scheduled for June 5 in Albuquerque. They would meet at the Indian Pueblo Cultural Center to discuss the next steps. They would bring their attorneys.

CHAPTER 6

Due to unforeseen events in the gallery, Laura didn't get her morning break today and after three hours on her feet discussing paintings to visitors, it was time for lunch. Laura knew she couldn't be late so made sure she wore her watch with the turquoise wristband. *Very Santa Fe,* she thought.

She went to the garden and found a quiet spot in the corner. She planned what she would do this week. Go to the library and research Indian Art, see a Flamenco performance. There's, also, the Piano Bar on Water St. *So much to do...*

Laura looked at her watch. Five more minutes. Better head back and freshen up. She didn't want to upset Anita again.

Back in the gallery, she took her place in the Santa Fe Art

Colony Collection. Within a few minutes a couple came in to look at the collection. They stopped and stared at a painting by Will Shuster. Laura approached them and asked if they were familiar with the artist. "We are from Denver. My wife is a college professor and I'm a real estate developer. We don't know about specific painters, but we know what we like. Can you tell us more about this artist?"

"Yes," Laura began. "This is Will Shuster. He came from back east as a war invalid. He came to New Mexico to recover from a lung ailment. He started painting portraits to pay the bills. The Museum of Fine Art opened in 1917 and gave artists a place to exhibit their art. Will Shuster painted the Santo Domingo Corn Dance, the Cross of the Martyr's Procession and other local cultural events. He was a co-creator of Zozobra, Old Man Gloom. It's a large marionette that gets burned in front of a large crowd. It's a yearly event during Santa Fe Fiesta in September. It's a time to burn your troubles away. He painted a mural of the Zozobra event, as well."

"That's very interesting. We will discuss this over lunch. What is your name?"

"Laura. Laura Barnes."

"We are the Ashtons. We will ask for you if we decide to make a purchase."

A few hours went by when the Ashtons returned. "We want to buy the painting, Laura. You sold us on Will Shuster."

Anita was in her office and Laura told the manager about the large transaction. When asked how they decided on this piece they said "Laura informed us of the artist's history and contribution to cultural life in Santa Fe. This was helpful in our decision making." replied Mr. Ashton.

Anita gathered the necessary information and told the buyers it could take up to an hour to coordinate with their bank in Denver. In the meantime, they were free to roam the garden or return in an hour. They chose to go to the garden.

Laura escorted them outside and strolled the grounds. They saw Mr. Canon talking to a gardener. She decided to introduce them. "Mr. Canon, I'd like you to meet some visitors. They just purchased a Will Shuster painting. They will take it back to Denver with them as soon as the transaction is processed. Mr. and Mrs. Ashton, this is the gallery owner, Mr. J.D. Canon." They shook hands.

"Well, hello there and welcome to my gallery. So, you like the Will Shuster painting? He co-created the Zozobra along with another artist, Gustave Baumann."

"Yes, Laura informed us of that, which is one of the reasons we wanted to purchase this piece." Mrs. Ashton replied.

"Well, Laura is one of my top salespeople." Canon said as he looked at Laura admiringly. "She's a teacher during the year, you know. I'm going to try to convince her to stay on."

Laura was surprised to hear this and blushed. "I do enjoy learning about the artists of the region and meeting interesting people from around the world."

Mrs. Ashton inserted, "Teaching is a noble profession, Laura. There's nothing to be embarrassed about. You may be good at art sales because you educate people. You're not pushy, just informative. We appreciate that in a salesperson."

Laura didn't hear Anita as she approached, "Your transaction is complete, Mr. and Mrs. Ashton. We wrapped the painting and it's ready for you." Mr. Canon thanked them for their business as Laura escorted them to the gallery exit where they said their good-byes.

Laura was feeling more confident as a salesperson and wondered what the owner meant by convincing her to stay on.

CHAPTER 7

June 7

Marc Bennett was sitting in his FBI office reading the local newspaper. He noticed the interview with a UNM professor saying that some galleries may be selling burial items from American Indian grave sites. Marc didn't know much about artifacts, but had heard of grave-diggers who looted items for profit. The professor was making a bold accusation. Marc wondered how these items were authenticated in order to be sold.

The office phone rang. "Marc, we just got an anonymous tip that there may be Indian burial items on display in art galleries around the southwest. One specific gallery in Santa Fe was mentioned, The J.D. Canon Gallery. Is this something you want to look into?" asked agent-in-charge Garland.

"Sir, why would this be an FBI matter?" asked agent Bennett.

"If there is looting of American Indian burial grounds, that's our jurisdiction because the items could be selling across state lines. When you get more information, you'll work with the local police. Do you want the assignment or not?"

"Yes, sir. There's something in the Albuquerque Times about this subject. It might be the same person giving us the tip. I've been to the gallery so I'll go undercover." Marc replied.

As he was checking his schedule for the next few days, the phone rang again. It was a law enforcement trainee he had met in Artesia, New Mexico, Martin Ross. They had both studied Advanced Forensic Techniques and exchanged contact information. Martin now worked for the Cherokee Nation Marshal Service in Oklahoma. Since Marc was with the FBI in Albuquerque, Martin reached out regarding a murder that took place in New Mexico.

"It's good to hear from you Martin. What can I help you with?"

"We have a case of a woman, Joyce Two Feathers Jordan. She's a Cherokee daughter and studied at the Institute of American Indian Arts. IAIA, for short. She lived in a dorm at the College of Santa Fe and had a part-time job at a gallery in town, The J.D. Canon Gallery. She was last seen May 15 at the gallery."

"I'm going to that gallery regarding another matter. What a coincidence." Marc replied.

"Good. Try to make a contact there and get any information you can on Joyce. The school president told the local police that she went to work on Friday afternoon, May 15, after her sculpture class and was found dead on campus grounds on Sunday, May 17. The toxicology report said she was poisoned. Cyanide. There were no signs of sexual assault. She had bruise marks on her arms and the backs of her legs."

Martin continued. "The County Coroner said the victim had been dead up to forty-eight hours before her body was found. Her roommate, Marie Ferris, told us she seemed fine when she left that day and glad to have the job. She had a yellow VW Bug she drove to work that was found near the gallery in a parking lot. Two tires were slashed. We don't know how she got back to campus. Question is: Was she killed on campus or by someone who drove her home? I'd appreciate your help on this, Marc."

"Can you text me the roommate's contact information? Who are you working with in the Santa Fe Police Department? I'll check in with them."

"I've spoken to Chief Romero about this." Martin replied.

"I'll get back to you, Martin." That conversation ignited

new interest for Marc in this prestigious Santa Fe art gallery. A young Cherokee art student is murdered after she leaves work at the gallery on Friday. An American Indian activist believes burial objects may have been stolen and are located at the same gallery. Two different crimes intersecting at the same location.

Marc cleared his schedule for the week and stopped in at agent Garland's office on his way out.

"Excuse me, sir. I just got a call from U.S. Marshal Ross from the Cherokee Nation regarding a murder victim. I knew him from training so he contacted me directly. The victim was Cherokee and went to school in Santa Fe. She worked at the J.D. Canon Gallery. Local police said the gallery manager was the last to see her alive. The victim's name is Joyce Two Feathers Jordan. Her body was found on the college campus. She was poisoned." Marc explained.

"Interesting. There's a lot to uncover at that gallery, agent. What did a college student know that would get her killed? Do you want a partner to work on the case?" Garland asked.

"Sir, I'll start to investigate on my own and keep you informed. In the mean-time, can you find an agent or researcher who is familiar with American Indian artifacts? There are museums in New Mexico that have researchers. There's the Museum of Indian Arts and Culture and the OAS research facility. If what we suspect is happening, we'll need the expertise to identify burial items. I know we have Pueblo and Navajo agents that can assist. Can you start putting a team together?" asked Marc.

"Yes, agent, good idea. We have some agents from area pueblos, both male and female." Garland replied. "You seem familiar with Santa Fe."

"Sir, I went sight-seeing as a tourist there recently. That's when I visited the J.D. Canon Gallery. There's an area called Gallery Row. Tourists and collectors go there, among other areas in town. That city's quite an art mecca. Too bad I have to visit again under these circumstances." Marc said as he prepared to leave.

"Agent Bennett, keep me informed and I'll get a team ready." Garland waved then got on the phone to coordinate a new mission.

CHAPTER 8

It took an hour to get to Santa Fe from the north side of Albuquerque. Marc parked on East Alameda and walked toward Canyon Road. On his way, he saw the young lady from the J.D. Canon Gallery. She had long brown wavy hair, which he had noticed when he first saw her. She was sitting on a bench along the river eating a sandwich. She had her shoes off and her feet were in the grass. He approached. "Hello, there. You're the salesperson who told me about lunch spots, aren't you?"

Laura gulped down her bite and wiped the crumbs from her mouth. "Yes, sir. Yes, I'm Laura. Laura Barnes." She cleared her throat and smiled at the man." So, which spot did you choose?"

"I chose the Purple Adobe. Meatloaf was great, like you

said. I never had anything like it. Regular meatloaf won't ever taste the same now." They laughed. "I was on my way back to the gallery. There's so much to see. So, how long have you worked there?"

"About three weeks. It's a summer job. I'm a school teacher and will return in August. I started college as an Art Major, so it's a nice break from teaching elementary school." Laura blushed as she said it. She almost forgot she was still a teacher.

"It must be an interesting place to work. Do others work part-time or just you?" Marc asked.

"Some staff are full-time. I'm here for the summer. Someone else was here in the spring. I didn't know her. She was a student at the IAIA." Laura replied.

Marc knew who Laura was referring to. Marc would have to find someone else at the gallery who knew the victim.

"I noticed there was quite a collection of American Indian items in the main office. Are they for sale?" Marc inquired.

"I'm told the collection is not for sale. It's Mr. Canon's private collection, so he deals with it. I overheard someone ask him the price of a shield, so I guess something is for sale for the right price." Laura said.

"Well, I'm going to stroll through a few other galleries, then make my way to the J.D. Canon Gallery. I'm Marc. Marc Bennett. Maybe I'll see you there, Laura."

Laura waved and watched him leave. He was a nice man

and she was flattered that he wanted to introduce himself. She looked at her watch. Five minutes late. Time to run! Anita told her she'd be docked if she was late again. She would say she was talking to a customer. She was considered a top salesperson now so Anita shouldn't be so harsh. Nevertheless, Laura walked quickly back to the gallery.

It was a few hours later when Marc entered the gallery. A woman greeted him. She looked to be in her late forties, with gray streaks in her primmed mid-length hair. The woman was dressed in a navy blazer and slacks. Two strands of white pearls adorned her neck. She was polite and business-like.

"My name is Carol. Let me know if I can answer any questions, Mr.?"

"Mr. Bennett. I have a property in Albuquerque and I'm considering a small outdoor bronze. Can you show me something?"

"Of course. Let's go to the garden." Carol replied.

"Tell me, Carol, what's it like working in a place like this? It's so distinctive with such a varied art collection."

"Well, Mr. Canon is collector of many things and a student of history, so he is always looking for special art. People from around the world visit the gallery. There's a small staff. The younger staff are usually part-time or just here for the summer. Some are teachers and some are students at local art schools. I've been here longer than most." Carol replied.

She continued. "Here are some bronzes you may like.

Of course, there are larger ones, life-size. I don't know your price-range so we can start here." They looked at a rabbit, an eagle in flight, a child reading a book. Marc knew he wasn't here to buy anything, but he needed to pretend to show interest.

"Let's keep looking." Marc said as he extended his conversation.

"You know, Carol, I heard on the local news about a student who was found dead on campus. I was surprised to hear that. I always thought Santa Fe was a quiet town." Marc inquired.

Carol looked saddened by the comment. "Well, yes, it generally is a quiet town. I believe you're referring to Joyce. She was an art student. She was a pretty young Cherokee Indian woman who studied sculpture at IAIA. It's so sad about her death. I have no idea what happened." Carol looked around and saw Anita nearby. She waved and pointed to the tall blonde woman. "That's the manager, Anita Boles."

Marc noticed that Carol became tense when she saw her manager nearby. They continued walking around the garden. Marc pretended to admire a sculpture. "Did you know Joyce?" Marc asked.

Carol was hesitant to answer then said "Yes, I did. She worked here part-time in the spring. I liked her. She was interested in the art and was good with customers. Mr.

Canon liked her. The manager spoke to the police a few days later. She was the last to see Joyce at the gallery. The police interviewed all of us." Carol wanted to change the subject. "Mr. Bennett, let's look at the larger sculptures, shall we?"

They looked at bronze animals and figures. Marc said he would let her know if he wanted to purchase one. "Thank you, Carol. I will consider one of these and will ask for you if I decide to make a purchase." He noticed the manager watching them. He nodded.

It was closing time, so Marc left the gallery. He decided to stroll around the side streets near Acequia Madre before returning to his car. Within minutes, he came across the young lady he saw by the river. "Well, hello again. Laura, is it?"

"Yes. I'm Laura." She blushed.

"I'm thinking of having dinner before I leave town. Would you care to join me?" asked Marc.

Laura's heart fluttered and she almost refused. Then, decided, why not? "I have a little time before I have to get home to take my dogs out. Shall we walk somewhere close by?"

"Yes, I saw a place up ahead near Camino del Monte Sol. It's not far from where I parked on the Alameda." Marc said.

They chatted about the gated entries to the homes, the adobe architecture of the southwest, the chili ristras hanging on the portals.

"So, what line of work are you in, Mr. Bennett? You seem very inquisitive."

"I'm doing research for background on a story I'm writing, Crime in the Historical Southwest. I'm writing for the New Mexico Historical Society." Marc made up a story, since he was undercover.

"That's interesting. Why are you visiting galleries for your research?" Laura asked.

"I'm actually spending most of my time in the library looking up old news articles. Going to galleries is more of a distraction from looking at microfilm." Marc thought that was a good excuse.

They got to the restaurant and sat on the portal, instead of going indoors. Both ordered chicken enchiladas "Christmas" and beer. Laura was feeling more relaxed with her dinner companion.

"I'll tell you, working at the gallery is a whole other world than I'm used to. I've worked with kids and parents, not high-end art and people from around the world." Laura stated. "My manager is so strict. She docks my pay if I'm late ten minutes from lunch. Don't get me wrong, I like working there."

"It looks like it's an interesting place to work, especially as a summer job. Are you required to make a certain number of sales?" Marc asked.

"I was told the part-timers don't have a quota. I've made sales and if you're wondering, no, I don't get paid extra for it. I enjoy learning about the artists so I can pass along the information to the customers. I have found that the more they know, the more likely they'll buy something." Laura said confidently.

Their food came and they savored the flavors of the red and green "Christmas" chile. The cold beer tasted good on this warm day. They discussed the food while watching people stroll by.

Marc continued. "You said people visit from around the world. Do many American Indians come through the gallery?"

"Not many that I've seen, but recently, three men came in. They were very serious-looking. They insisted on seeing Mr. Canon's private collection. I was in the adjacent room and didn't hear everything, but the owner eventually let them look in his office. The office door is usually open. Now that I think about it, when American Indians arrive, the owner or manager try to keep the office door closed."

Laura continued. "Of course, some are sculptors and painters who do business with the gallery."

"When I visited the gallery the office door was open and I noticed a large collection. Why would the management want the door closed to Indigenous visitors?" Marc inquired.

"Well, based on the responses of the three men who visited, I can only presume they were concerned about something they saw." Laura replied.

"Laura, I've seen in the local news that a student was found dead on the college campus here. Her name was Joyce Two Feathers Jordan. I heard she worked at J.D. Canon Gallery." Marc said.

"Yes, I know. The police came to the gallery on my first day there, May 25. They interviewed all of us. The manager admitted she fired Joyce because she didn't meet the sales quota and didn't know what happened after Joyce left the gallery." Laura said.

"That's interesting, Laura, because you just told me the part-timers don't have a sales quota. Why would Joyce be fired for that?" Marc pressed.

"You're right, Marc. That's odd." Laura was curious now.

"Maybe you can ask other staff who's been there longer about the sales quota? Sounds like you're safe if you've been selling, but Joyce wasn't." Marc said.

"Marc. I think I'd better head home. I'm a few blocks over on Acequia Madre."

"Let me walk you." Marc paid the bill and they proceeded to Camino del Monte Sol and over to Acequia Madre. They stopped at Pena Court.

"Here's my street. Thank you for dinner and walking me home, Marc."

"My pleasure. Can I give you my phone number?" Marc wanted to see this woman again and not just at the gallery.

Laura smiled. "OK, Marc. Good night."

Laura head to her casita and unlocked the gate. Her dogs howled anxiously as she entered. "OK, fellas, I'm home. Let's take you for a walk."

As she walked the quiet streets, Laura needed to check her emotions. She was glad to have met a nice man who seemed smart and was certainly handsome. She felt a friendship forming. She wasn't anxious for a new romance, so she'd be cautious. It was fun to explore area restaurants and she wanted to make new friends. It was getting lonely going places by herself.

She, also, wondered about Joyce. It was unsettling to know a former staff member was killed and that American Indians were suspicious of the owner's artifact collection. She decided to be more observant and would talk to Carol when she had a chance.

Walking helped calm her as she enjoyed the company of her four-legged companions.

CHAPTER 9

June 8

After taking a hot shower and turning in early the night before, Laura felt ready for another day. She would find the chance to talk to Carol and learn more about Joyce.

Laura clocked in at nine, put her sack lunch in the fridge and went to her station. Since there were no visitors yet, she reached for the binder and continued reading about the lives of the artists.

Laura gazed at the large Baumann woodcut before her. She loved the blue sky and billowy clouds. She imagined what a fun friendship Baumann and Shuster must have had in the early days of Santa Fe's art scene. Together, they created a larger than life-size puppet and had a party to watch it burn.

She became startled by a man's voice "Laura, I want to congratulate you on the Shuster sale."

"Oh, you're welcome, Mr. Canon. They were nice people to work with and I just told them what I knew about the artist."

"As a bonus, I want to give you this pendant." He handed her a blue lapis stone set in silver." I think you should work for me full-time. What do you say?" he asked.

"Oh, thank you. Blue is my favorite color." Laura said as she admired the stone. "I don't know, sir. My principal is expecting me and I'd miss my students. It would be a big decision for me." She became distracted by visitors and directed her attention to them. Canon left the room.

Laura spoke to the visitors, but no one seemed serious about buying. She was, at first, rattled by Mr. Canon's question, then dismissed the idea. She thought he probably said that to all the young women.

Lunchtime came and Laura head to the garden. She saw Carol walking with a customer. She approached and whispered to Carol, "Can I talk to you when you're finished with your customer? I have a question. I'll be on the bench having my lunch.

"OK, but it might be a while." Carol replied.

Carol returned twenty minutes later. "Anita is processing the sale so I have a few minutes. What's on your mind?"

"Carol, I'm curious about Joyce. Can you tell me more about her? I know she was a student at the IAIA. Why was she fired? I heard Anita tell the police it was because she didn't meet the sales quota. I was told when I applied there was no quota for part-time staff." Laura inquired.

"I was surprised to hear she was fired for that reason because Joyce was good with customers, like you are. She made sales, too." Carol looked pensive. "I did notice she started asking Mr. Canon questions about his private collection. He doesn't like to be questioned, especially by staff. He expects loyalty. Joyce was concerned about something in her last few days, but didn't talk to me about it. I liked Joyce. She was a sweet girl and a long way from home. It's so sad." Carol looked around to be sure no one was nearby.

Carol continued. "Anita told us not to discuss Joyce, remember? There's something that's been bothering me, though. About a week after Joyce's death, just before you started, I saw Anita adjusting her collar in the bathroom. I noticed a copper necklace under her blouse. I pretended to be looking at my hair, but I saw it. It was a star inside a circle."

"Why did that bother you?" asked Laura.

"I saw Joyce wearing one just like it. She wore it every day. She said it reminded her of home on the Cherokee Nation in Oklahoma. I don't know why Anita would be wearing it. I never told the police, because Anita was with me when I was being questioned." Carol stood up and straightened her jacket. "I'd better go now."

"Carol. Thanks for telling me. I'm just curious." Laura said.

Laura was starting to wonder about Anita's behavior. Carol was obviously worried about Anita overhearing their conversations. Some things didn't make sense, like the sales quota as the reason Joyce was fired. Laura had to find the copper necklace. It could have been Joyce's.

Laura returned to her station after lunch. A man with an Italian accent came in and stared at the Baumann woodcut. "Can I help you with something?"

"I love the blue sky and lovely clouds. So real, just like the sky today. I'm visiting from Rome and I have never seen such blue skies!" the man said in an Italian accent.

"Yes, the air is very clear at this elevation. There are few pollutants and the sky is the brightest blue I've ever seen. I'm from the Midwest and I couldn't believe my eyes when I first got here." Laura made conversation.

"Do you know about this artist, Baumann?"

Laura recalled what she had read earlier. "Yes, he's from Chicago where he studied art, then went to Germany to study print-making. He lived in New York awhile before coming to New Mexico. He visited Santa Fe and got a job at the museum building studio furniture. He moved to a studio on Canyon

Road, where he made wood-cuts, such as this one. He, also, carved marionettes. He's the co-creator of a large marionette called Old Man Gloom. Every year, the puppet is built and then burned during Santa Fe Fiesta. It's a huge spectacle!"

"Well, young lady, that is very interesting and I'm afraid, I must have this wood cut! I love the clouds and I will always think of New Mexico when I am in Rome. Mi chiamo Gianni. My name is Gianni. What is your name?"

"My name is Laura. Laura Barnes. It's so nice to meet you, Gianni." They shook hands." I'll take you to the office and the manager, Anita, will handle your transaction. Follow me, please."

When they got to the front office, Laura introduced Gianni and said he wanted to purchase the Baumann woodcut. Anita got up from her desk and said she would get the artwork and write up an invoice. While waiting, Gianni asked to use the restroom. Laura was alone in Anita's office. This was her chance.

Laura looked around the room and saw shelves of pottery and books. There were photos of Anita with the Canon family on vacation. She stood by the desk and slid open the middle desk drawer, just pens and invoice pad. She grabbed a pen and slid it in her pocket. She quietly opened each drawer. When she got to the bottom left drawer, she felt it tug. Something was stuck. She pulled at the drawer and saw a scarf. She lifted the scarf and a copper necklace fell out. A circle with a star carved in black. She put the scarf back in the drawer.

Laura heard people talking. She scooped up the necklace in her hand and closed the drawer just as Anita and Gianni approached the door. She slid the necklace in her back pocket. She turned around to pretend she was looking at a painting on the wall behind the desk. The quick turn caused her to bump the computer. She steadied herself, heart racing. She tried to remain calm. Unless there were hidden cameras in the room, no one saw her.

Anita entered with the artwork. The customer followed. "Laura, you can go back to your section now. I'll write up this transaction."

"Grazie, Laura, grazie!" Gianni said.

"Prego. You're welcome." Laura wished him well on his trip back to Rome. She returned to her section and let out a deep sigh. She made sure the necklace was hidden in her pocket and thought of what to do next. She had another hour to go before closing time. She decided that after work she would go to the downtown library and research Cherokee jewelry.

She was glad to have another big sale, but that joy soon led to suspicion. Why would Joyce part with her cherished necklace and why Anita would have it?

Just then, the gallery owner entered the room. "Laura,

Laura you did it again. You made a big sale! There's no question this is the work you should be doing. You are good at sales because you're teaching the customers to buy what they love. Don't you see? Come on. I'll pay you a very good salary. What do you say?"

"Mr. Canon, I appreciate your offer. Can you give me a few weeks to think about it? Have you discussed it with Anita?" Laura asked.

"No, no. I don't make these offers lightly and it's my decision. I will give you one week then the offer expires." Canon pressed.

Anita walked in as the owner was leaving the room. "Laura, congratulations on another sale. I can see that Mr. Canon is quite pleased with you. Did I just hear him ask you to stay on past the summer?" Anita continued. "You know, I do the scheduling and we already have enough full-time staff. Sometimes Mr. Canon says things without discussing with me first. I do the hiring and the firing."

"Oh, yes, I docked your pay for being late from lunch the other day." Anita turned abruptly and left. She didn't like the attention Laura was getting from the owner. She only hired the school teacher because she was na·ive.

Laura was getting perturbed by Anita's sarcasm and the owner's pressure to quit her teaching job. She didn't know who to listen to, the owner or the manager.

After work, Laura walked quickly to the Plaza downtown. She wanted to get to the library before closing time at six. She walked down Alameda St. to Old Santa Fe Trail, past La Fonda Hotel and over to Washington St. The main library was still open. She went to the Information Desk and asked for the section on Indian jewelry. She went to the second floor and searched for Cherokee art. Laura found a book on famous jewelers and head to the nearest table to sit down.

Many of the jewelers worked in copper and the most often-used design was the Cherokee Star. This was a seven-pointed star representing the seven clans of the Cherokee Nation. Laura took the necklace out of her back pocket and laid it on the page. She compared the designs and found it was, in fact, the Cherokee Star.

There was a mark on the underside of the necklace. This would be the artist's stamp. She would look that up later. For now, she would head home and think of what to do with this necklace.

CHAPTER 10

June 9

The next day, Laura kept busy at the gallery as tourists flowed through all the rooms. She didn't have much time to read or talk to Carol. Anita only spoke to tell her when to go on break and to lunch. Laura was hoping Anita didn't realize the necklace was gone. Laura kept it wrapped in a napkin inside the pocket of her blazer.

Keeping the copper necklace nearby made Laura feel close to Joyce. *I would have liked her.*

After work, Laura decided to walk to the Plaza. She was feeling guilty about taking the necklace, but some things about Joyce's death were not adding up. Laura realized she was acting like a sleuth now. She never thought she had the instincts, but she felt compelled to get answers.

An innocent woman may have been killed by someone at the gallery. *Why? What should I do with the necklace? Should I go to the police?*

Laura head home, walking past the Cathedral and its parking lot, then over to Alameda. Her feet were aching, having been standing most of the day, then walking downtown. She found a bench near the river and sat down to rest her feet.

After a few minutes she saw a car drive by slowly. A woman was staring at her. It was Anita. She waved and yelled "Do you want a ride, Laura?"

"No, thank you, I'm fine." Laura yelled back.

"Come on, I insist! I'll go around the block and come back for you." Anita said.

Laura waved her on and shook her head. "No, Anita, I don't need a ride. I'm fine, really." She didn't want to take a ride from Anita.

Just then, she saw a black Jeep approaching with a blonde-haired man at the wheel. He slowed down and called out "Laura, is that you?" It was Marc.

"Yes, it's me!" she waved happily.

Marc pulled his Jeep over along the church parking lot and got out. He walked across the street and over to the bench. "Funny, seeing you here. I was just going to get dinner. Do you want to come with? I'd like to revisit the Purple Adobe."

"Oh, that would be nice. I'm actually quite famished. Yes,

let's go!" They got in the Jeep just as Anita's car came back around.

Marc found a quiet corner table in the back room of the busy restaurant. He wanted a quieter setting than the bustling chatter in the front section. "So, what's new since I saw you last?"

Laura looked around the room to be sure no one from the gallery was there before speaking. "After we talked, I decided to ask another staff member at the gallery more about Joyce, the student who died. We were told by the manager not to discuss the matter, but Carol was willing to talk to me." Laura bent in toward Marc.

"I feel like I can confide in you." Laura said.

Marc confessed. "Laura, I need to tell you something first. I'm not a writer. I'm in law enforcement."

"Law enforcement? What kind?" Laura was surprised.

"I'm with the FBI, Albuquerque office. Does that bother you?" Marc asked.

"Actually, I think it's a good thing." Laura let out a sigh and smiled.

The waitress approached with water and took their orders. Both wanted the Santa Fe meatloaf and a beer.

"I don't suppose you want to tell me why you're visiting galleries here, do you?" Laura wondered.

Marc paused before responding. "Well, I'm actually investigating Joyce's death. The Cherokee Nation asked me to look into it. I'm coordinating with the local police." He looked around the room before speaking. "I'm undercover, Laura, so don't mention this to anyone. Can I count on you to do that?"

"Yes, Marc. I'm really glad you told me because I was thinking about talking to the police. I can talk to you instead." Laura felt somewhat relieved now.

Their meal came and they switched the topic to food. "This meatloaf is like nothing I've ever tasted. It's delicious!" Marc said between bites.

"New Mexico food is so unique." Laura said. "It must be the creative use of chile. Who would have thought to mix chile and walnuts in meatloaf? They put chile in everything here." She sipped her beer and cooled her throat from the spicy meal.

"So, what did Carol tell you, Laura?"

"She said Joyce had been concerned her last few days, after asking Mr. Canon about his artifact collection. Though the owner liked Joyce, he didn't like staff asking him questions. We were told Joyce was fired because she didn't meet the sales quota, but Carol said Joyce made sales and was good with the customers. When I applied, Anita said part-timers didn't have a sales quota. So, we really don't know why Joyce was fired. Carol told me something else, Marc." Laura finished her meal and looked around the room.

"She noticed Anita wearing a necklace, the same necklace

Joyce wore every day to remind her of home. It was a copper circle with a black star in the center. Carol noticed it when they were freshening up in the restroom. This was a week after Joyce's death, just before I started. She didn't tell the police because Anita was in the room when they questioned her." Laura was speaking more softly now, since she didn't want anyone else to hear what she was about to say.

"This is interesting, Laura." Marc said.

The waitress collected their plates. "Dessert anyone?" she asked.

"How about two apple pies?" Marc asked and Laura agreed.

Laura continued. "Marc, I went into Anita's office yesterday. It was the perfect chance for me to look around. I went through her drawers and found the necklace. I took it. I went to the library after work to research Cherokee jewelry. The necklace is the Cherokee Star. I have it right here." Laura took it out of her pocket and opened the napkin.

"Marc, I'm so glad you drove by when you did. Anita saw me sitting there and wanted to give me a ride home. I waved her on. She came back around right after I got in your car. I'm feeling very uncomfortable around her. I hope she doesn't know I took the necklace. I don't usually steal other people's things." Laura said.

The waitress approached with their dessert, so Laura covered the necklace. They paused their conversation and smiled until they were alone. Marc leaned in.

"Laura, you took a big risk talking to Carol and taking that necklace. It may upset you, but I will tell you something about Joyce's death." Marc moved closer to Laura as he explained. "She was poisoned. She had a yellow VW Bug with two slashed tires parked in the lot across from the gallery. The police don't know if she was killed on campus or by someone who drove her home."

"Oh, that poor girl." Laura shook her head. "Marc, what should I do with this?" Laura pointed to the wrapped necklace.

"I'd like to keep it as evidence. There should be prints on it." He placed it in his coat pocket. "Your prints are in the system, being a teacher. We can compare Joyce's prints. I'm not sure about Anita's. Maybe she was finger-printed to get the gallery position. Laura, can you try to get something with her prints on it?"

"Oh, wait." She dug in her pocket using a napkin and presented a pen. "I took this pen from Anita's desk, too. I'm not sure why." Laura said.

"Good work, Laura. I'll check this for Anita's prints and compare them to the necklace." Marc told her.

"Can I tell you something else, Marc? It's been on my mind and I haven't told anyone." She touched his arm.

He put his hand over hers and said "Of course, Laura."

"It was my first day on the job, May 25th. The police

came to interview everyone about Joyce. After lunch, the owner, Mr. Canon asked me to look at something in his den. I couldn't say no, right?" Laura sipped her water. "Well, there was a pool table with a white sheet laid out. On it was a human skeleton. Human remains with dirt still on the bones! It smelled awful and it made me sick to my stomach."

"Yes, that would be upsetting, Laura. Did he say where the remains came from?" Marc asked.

"He said he dug them up on his land outside Santa Fe. He found them under some stones. He was smiling so proudly when he showed it to me. I never saw anything like it and got nauseous. I was late getting back and the manager was upset with me. Why would someone have human bones on their premises?" Laura asked.

"It's very unusual. I'm glad you told me, Laura." Marc's mind was racing with this new information. "Do you know where his land is?"

"He said it was out near Pecos National Monument. It's vacant land." Laura said. They finished dessert. "It's been quite a day. I'm ready to go home." Laura said.

Marc drove Laura home. Before exiting the Jeep, Laura asked "Marc, am I in trouble for taking that necklace?"

"Not in this incident. I doubt that you're in the habit of stealing, are you?"

"Of course not! I'm a school teacher. I teach kids to know

the difference between right and wrong. It seems some people forget that when they grow up." Laura defended herself.

"Yes, they do. That's why law enforcement stays busy. I'll see you soon, Laura. Good night." Marc drove off. He had more stops to make.

Laura took her dogs for their evening walk after a long eventful day.

She had just gotten back to her casita when she heard the phone ring. "Laura, it's mom. Your dad and I are wondering how you're doing since I last spoke to you?"

"Hi, mom. Well, I've been doing good with sales at the gallery and now the owner wants me to work full-time. He gave me a week to decide."

"You're a teacher, Laura. You always wanted to be a teacher and you're good at it. The kids love you. Teaching is your profession." Her mother insisted.

"I know, but Mr. Canon said he'd pay me a higher salary. I meet people from all over the world. I'm learning a lot about art, too." Laura explained.

"Laura, this is your father speaking. I want you to stay in teaching. It is a calling and you're good at it. You can work in the gallery during the summer and on weekends. If not this one, then another. There are a lot of galleries in that town. Your mother and I are very worried about you."

Her mother came back on the line. "It's been a tough year

for you, getting divorced, relocating on your own and being away from your family. You're very vulnerable right now, so you need to be careful with your decisions. If it's money you need, we can send some to hold you over until you get on your feet."

"I'll let you know if I need money. Since you both feel so strongly about it, I won't commit to anything yet. Of course, the manager didn't seem keen on the idea and she does the scheduling. The owner told me one thing and she told me another. I really don't know who to believe." Laura admitted.

Her mother continued. "That's even more reason not to resign from teaching. You don't know if they're even serious about the job offer. Don't be pressured, Laura. This is your career you're talking about."

"I'm so glad you called tonight, mom. Say goodnight to dad, for me."

Laura wondered how her parents had an uncanny way of knowing she needed them from twelve hundred miles away. It must be an intuitive sense.

She settled in for the night.

CHAPTER 11

Before leaving town, Marc called Marie Ferris and introduced himself. He asked if he could meet her in an hour at the dormitory. She agreed.

On his way, he went to the Santa Fe Police Department to talk to Chief Romero. The Chief was in. Marc introduced himself as an agent of the Albuquerque bureau.

"Yes, agent Garland called me earlier today." The Chief stood and shook Marc's hand. "You're here looking into the case of the college student, Joyce Two Feathers Jordan. What can I help you with, agent?"

"I wanted to get an update on the investigation thus far. The Cherokee Nation

U.S. Marshal agent, Martin Ross, told me you had an autopsy and toxicology done. Can I see a copy of the report?" Marc asked.

The Chief pulled the reports up on the computer and made print-outs. Marc scanned the pages. "So, cause of death: cyanide poisoning. No signs of sexual assault or rape. Bruising under the arms and back of the legs. The body had been dead up to forty-eight hours before being discovered. There were some bite marks on soft flesh, most likely from scavenging animals. What about her clothes? Were they torn? Did police find any jewelry on the victim? Any shoe prints around the crime scene?"

"No jewelry found on or around the scene. From bruise marks, it appears the victim was dragged through gravel and grass. She was shielded in the tall grass, where hikers found her. There were shoe prints, but hard to tell if they were from the suspect, since the area was grassy." The Chief explained.

"Have you or your officers visited the roommate or searched the dorm room?" Marc inquired.

"My officer got some preliminary information from the roommate, Marie Ferris.

They looked in the dorm room, but found nothing of interest to the case. They closed off the room."

"Did you search Joyce's car, the VW Bug? Is it impounded?" Marc asked.

"We searched the car and dusted for prints. Only Joyce's prints were found. The car is impounded as evidence, for now."

"Well, Chief. I want to share some new information

I learned today. I spoke to a gallery staff member, Laura Barnes, who gave me something that could help the case." Marc pulled the napkin out of his jacket and unwrapped the necklace. "This is a necklace another staffer said the victim wore daily. Laura became suspicious and found this, took this, from the manager's desk drawer yesterday."

Marc continued. "After some research, Laura confirmed it is the Cherokee Star. Our victim, Joyce, was Cherokee. I'm taking this to forensics tonight to check for prints. We should have Laura's prints in the system, since she's a teacher during the year. We have the victim's prints. We'll see if we have Anita's prints in the system." Marc took out another item wrapped in a napkin. "Laura took a pen from the manager's desk, as well. We'll compare these prints to those on the necklace."

"Well, this is helpful, agent. It's good you have an informant at the gallery, but tell her to be careful. She's playing detective and could get hurt. Let me know if the necklace was Joyce's. You didn't have a warrant to take this, but a concerned citizen took it. That should hold up in court." The Chief replied.

"Another thing, Chief. Our office got a tip that American Indian burial items may be in the owner's possession. Canon says the items aren't for sale. A local professor claims the items were stolen from Indigenous graves. If so, they could be selling across state lines and that's FBI business. In addition, our informant said she was shown human remains in a room on the gallery premises. The owner admitted he dug them up on his property outside of town. Canon told her he found items next to the remains, too." Marc explained.

Chief Romero said. "So, the FBI is here for two possible crimes involving the same gallery. J.D. Canon has been here awhile and is supposed to have a good reputation. His art sells for high dollars. We have to be sure about this, agent."

"Yes, I'm aware. I suggest you not share this part of the investigation with your officers yet, since I'm working undercover. In a small town, officers may talk and word gets back to the gallery. Do you know what I mean, Chief?"

"Yes, I do. Keep me informed agent." The Chief replied.

"I'm going to the dormitory to interview the roommate, Marie Ferris. I'll let you know if I learn anything new. It's good to meet you, Chief." They shook hands.

The sun was setting and the sky was lit with an orange glow as Marc drove to the campus. He turned off Rodeo Road then onto Richards Avenue. On open winding roads he drove towards the campus grounds. On the left, he noticed yellow crime scene tape marking off a small area. He pulled his Jeep onto the shoulder and got out. It was near dusk as he walked over to the posts stretched with tape. Marc walked slowly while looking at the ground. There were tall grassy areas, but he noticed a long strip of matted grass coming from the road. The body was dragged here.

He went back to the Jeep and proceeded to the women's

dormitory of the IAIA. He met Marie by the front desk. He introduced himself to the person on duty and showed his badge. They walked up to the third floor. Marie had moved to another room since her roommate's death.

They approached a door with red crime scene tape across it. "Here's our room." Marc put on rubber gloves and opened the door. Marie pointed to a section of the room marked off with yellow crime scene tape. "That was Joyce's area."

Marc stepped under the tape. He saw shelves of books, photos of family dressed in Cherokee regalia, notebooks and a sketchbook. He flipped through the books.

Nothing looked of interest. He opened the sketchbook and sat at what had been Joyce's desk. There were drawings of shapes for sculptures, landscapes, flowers, and people.

Marie watched from the doorway as the agent browsed through the sketchbook. "Joyce loved to sketch things around her. She was very observant."

Notes were written on some pages. Marc noticed on one page, there were drawings of baskets. On another page was a drawing of a flute, a primitive looking flute with something hanging from it, like strands of cloth. A word next to the baskets read *Stolen?* Next to the flute read *Burial item?*

Marc stood up and said "I'd like to take this sketchbook, Marie. It may help in our investigation. Thank you for meeting me today. I'm sorry for your loss." Marc shook Marie's hand and saw the tears in her eyes. He taped the door closed.

It was dark now as he drove back towards Rodeo Road. The main road to and from the campus was nearly deserted. There were few street lights and open spaces were blackened by the night. Marc could see that it was a clever place to hide a body and a good way to confuse the police.

CHAPTER 12

As Marc drove south on the interstate, he thought of what he had to do. He would call his contact at the Cherokee Nation and send him a photo of the necklace to share with Joyce's family. They could confirm if it was hers.

He pulled over to get gas and called the FBI office from his car phone. He spoke to agent-in-charge, Garland. "What do you have, agent?"

"Sir, I've got the victim's necklace from a contact at the gallery who found it in the manager's possession. I have a pen used by the manager. I'm bringing them in tonight to check for prints. I got the victim's sketchbook from the roommate. There were notes and sketches that may be tied to the artifact collection."

Marc continued. "We know the victim was poisoned and her tires were slashed. She had a yellow VW Bug in a lot across from the gallery. I think we should check cameras around the lot for the dates May 15 to May 17, when the body was found. Maybe we'll get an ID on whoever slashed the tires. Maybe Joyce went back to the gallery to get a ride. The manager was the last to see her leave."

"Ok, agent. I'll call Chief Romero to access the cameras in the parking lot for those dates."

"Another thing, sir. My gallery contact said the owner showed her a human skeleton. He described it as a Native American male. He said he found items with it. More artifacts? He dug it up on his property outside of Santa Fe, near the Pecos Monument."

"We'll meet in the morning, agent. By then, we should get news from forensics."

Marc got back on the highway and thought about what he knew, so far. His office got a tip that the gallery owner had stolen artifacts belonging to Indigenous people. The Albuquerque Times newspaper quoted UNM Professor John Buffalo, saying the same thing. From what Marc could see, the owner's office was filled with Native American items. Laura said the collection was not for sale, but had overheard price being discussed for one item.

Management didn't want Indigenous people looking at the collection and closed the office door when possible. Now,

Marc saw a connection to the murder of the Cherokee art student. The notes in Joyce's sketchbook alluded to stolen items. She must have known.

He drove carefully down the steep La Bajada Hill past Pueblos and towards Rio Rancho. Big city lights sprawled out ahead. Traffic picked up and Marc had to stay alert. He got to the FBI field office and head to the lab.

"Marc, what do you have for me?" asked the technician.

"I need you to check this necklace and pen for prints. First, take photos of the front and back of the necklace, then send them to my computer. I think the murder suspect took this from the victim and wore it, like a souvenir. I'd like a rush on this, if you can. There may be three sets of prints."

Marc stopped at the Break Room before heading to his office. He needed some coffee before calling the Marshal.

After settling in his leather chair and accessing the photos on his computer, he called Marshal Ross. "Martin, I have an update for you on Joyce Two Feathers Jordan. A gallery staffer found a copper necklace in the manager's office that she thinks belonged to Joyce. Another staffer saw the manager wearing it a week after Joyce's death."

"What did it look like, Marc?"

"It's copper. There's a circle with a black star inside. The star has seven points. I'm sending you the photos now."

"It sounds like the Cherokee Star. The seven points represent the seven clans. I'll print out the photos and show them to Joyce's family to identify. There should be an artist's stamp on the back of the circle. A lot of jewelers stamp their work to identify it as authentic. Her parents may know the jeweler." Ross explained.

"Another thing, Martin. I went to Joyce's dorm room and met her roommate. I have Joyce's sketchbook. I guess the police didn't see anything relevant since they didn't know we're investigating stolen burial items. I noticed some sketches with notations written next to them. I'll take pictures of the pages in question. One sketch shows small baskets with the word *stolen, question mark.* Another sketch is a flute with strands of cloth hanging from one side with the words *burial item, question mark.* Does that mean anything to you?"

"The Cherokee people are known for basket weaving. There's a tradition of placing small burial baskets with the deceased. The flute could be a Warrior's Flute. It would have six holes and strands of leather. It's buried with the warrior. Sound to me like Joyce recognized these items in Mr. Canon's collection."

"Could it be that someone had her killed before she reported it to authorities? I'll look at the photos and talk to the family. I'll follow up with you in the morning, Marc."

"Sure enough, Martin. Good night."

Marc sent agent-in-charge Garland a message. "We have two possible crimes involving staff at the Canon Gallery. First,

J.D. Canon may be looting Indigenous graves and ruins and trafficking across state lines. Second, someone at the gallery may have killed the young woman, Joyce, a Cherokee Indian. Based on sketches in her notebook, she suspected some of Canon's artifacts were stolen."

Marc decided to go home and get some rest. He would resume the investigation in the morning.

Across New Mexico this night the Pueblo Council, Navajo Nation Council, and the Apache Councils were in session. The members discussed what to do about the looting of Indigenous burial sites and the sale of sacred items. The name of a gallery in Santa Fe was the main point of interest, since Professor Buffalo of UNM and two Pueblo Elders personally saw items in question at this gallery. There was discussion that other galleries or individuals across the country could be selling stolen items to collectors.

The Councils emphasized that laws had to be enacted and be enforced to prevent looting of graves and ruins, as well as the sale of artifacts. One recent law imposed fines and prison time if caught looting on Indian land and public lands.

This law was proven difficult to enforce on the open lands of the reservations.

The Pueblo Council decided to hold a protest at the J.D. Canon Gallery. They contacted leaders of the Navajo and Apache Nations for agreement. The Tribal leaders agreed they had to show unity. They would bring their attorneys. Singers would come with their drums. The local press would be notified about the date and time of the protest. The protesters would demand the return of their sacred burial items.

CHAPTER 13

June 10

At the FBI office this morning, Garland called a meeting with Marc Bennett and a team of other agents. Marc looked around to see some familiar faces. Celia Martinez and Jerry Roybal were from nearby Pueblos, one agent was from the Navajo Nation, Ben Yazzie. Marc had worked with him on a case in Ramah.

Agent-in-charge Garland began. "There is a Santa Fe art gallery under suspicion of looting graves and selling across state lines. I need someone to go undercover who can identify these items. Marc Bennett has been there so I'll let him tell you more about it."

"Good morning, everyone. The gallery owner, J.D.

Canon, has been in business for many years, so we have to be sure before we get a warrant to search. Canon's office door was open when I visited twice, but he tries to close it off to Indigenous visitors. We need someone who can identify burial items, but doesn't look Indigenous."

A woman raised her hand. "I'm a researcher at the Office of Archeological Studies or OAS, for short. Agent Garland asked me to assist on your case. I can identify American Indian burial items. I'll pretend to be a collector to gain access to the office. I don't think anyone in the gallery would recognize me, but I can wear a wig, just in case. My name is Maureen Jansen."

Marc looked at agent Garland and they shook their heads in agreement. "Good to meet you, Ms. Jansen. When can you get there?" Marc asked.

"I'll leave right after this meeting. I just have to stop off to get a wig, first. Should I try to purchase an artifact, agent?" Maureen replied.

"Good idea. Pay cash, so they don't get your real name. The FBI will reimburse you. Be aware of the manager, Anita Boles. She's the tall one with long blonde hair. She's a suspect in the murder of a young staffer, Joyce Two Feathers Jordan. We think, based on Joyce's drawings, that she recognized stolen items. We're working on getting a warrant to search Anita's home and vehicle. Agent Garland, did you get word from Chief Romero about camera footage at the parking lot?"

"Not yet. They have a small staff in that department, so things move slower than we'd like. I'll check my computer again shortly. We did get a report on the necklace. It had Joyce's prints on them, as well as your informant's. Anita's prints matched prints on the pen."

Garland continued. "I put this team together because we have two possible crimes involving the same gallery. When Ms. Jansen reports back, we'll know for sure about the burial items. Once confirmed, I'll get a warrant to search the gallery and the premises. I'd like Ben Yazzi from the Navajo Nation and Celia Martinez, from Cochiti Pueblo to collect the burial items and inventory them along with Ms. Jansen. Agent Williams will have a truck ready on stand-by to load items you retrieve. The truck will have packing materials, tables and a ladder, if needed."

Marc spoke up. "There's a man in shipping, Tom. Also, the wife and two children live on the premises. Agent Janelle, you'll search the residence and question the family. Jerry, you'll search the den and assist Janelle. A full skeleton was viewed by my informant. It was last seen on the pool table in the den. Take any suspected items from the living area to the den for identification."

"Any questions?" Garland asked.

Ben asked "What will happen to the burial items once taken from the gallery?"

"They will be put in a secure location to be returned to the American Indian tribes." Garland responded.

Marc looked at Maureen. "Good luck, Ms. Jansen."

The researcher left and Garland concluded the meeting. It was nine thirty a.m. The agents dispersed to other areas of the building as they waited to go on their assignment. Marc sat at his desk. His phone rang. It was Marshal Ross.

"Marc, Joyce's family identified the necklace as the one they gave her before she came to Santa Fe. They know the artist by his stamp. She always wore it and would never have given it away."

"And Marc, those sketches you sent on the computer are Cherokee burial items, like I thought. Joyce recognized them. I'm coming to New Mexico. I'll let you know when I arrive." Marshal Ross hung up.

The redhead found a wig store near the hospital that was frequented by cancer patients who had lost their hair. She remembered that her mother had once gone there. Maureen purchased a long-haired brunette wig, much different from her short red hair. She put it on snug and looked in the mirror. She barely recognized herself. Good!

She already had on a two-piece suit, so didn't have to change clothes. Maureen looked in her purse. She had her checkbook and credit card. She needed cash. A stop at the ATM would get her five hundred dollars. She decided she might need more. Before getting on the Interstate, Maureen stopped at another branch ATM.

On the drive north, Maureen thought of her act. She'd have a slight southern drawl and say she was from New Orleans. She'd look around the gallery and stop by the office. If the door wasn't open, she'd ask to see the owner, J.D. Then, she'd put on the charm.

The researcher parked in the lot across from the gallery. She put on more lipstick and powdered her nose. She adjusted her rings and bracelets, then unbuttoned the top buttons of her blouse. She sprayed a bit of cologne. She was ready.

Once inside the gallery, a tall woman with blonde hair greeted her and asked if she needed assistance. Maureen said she'd like to look around first. She went from room to room, admiring the paintings and sculpture. She was admiring a painting by A. Dasburg, when a man approached. She noticed a scent of musty cologne in the air.

"Well, hello there. Welcome to my gallery." He held out his hand and Maureen put on a smile, shaking his hand lightly. "I'm J.D. Canon."

"It's so nice to meet you, sir. I've heard about this gallery and just had to visit." She responded in a southern drawl. Canon seemed smitten with the visitor.

"Where are you from, Miss...." He asked.

"Oh, I'm from New Orleans. I'm Susan Jennings." She kept smiling.

"Can I show you around, Miss Jennings?" Canon asked.

"Well, that would be so very kind of you." She gushed.

He escorted her past the office and out to the garden. They spoke of the dry New Mexico climate compared to the humid air of New Orleans. She admired the flowers. Canon asked "Are you looking for something special to take back home with you?"

"Well, actually, Mr. Canon, I'm a fan of old Native American antiquities. I just love the craftsmanship of some of those things. For instance, the old moccasins, you know with all the beads, or those rings of claws they wore around their necks and those old flutes. Imagine, how could they could carve a musical instrument like that? I mean, what kind of tools did they have way back then? I'm just fascinated with those old things." The visitor was laying on the charm and J.D. was falling for it.

"Miss Jennings, why don't we go to my office? I have something you might like. It's my personal collection."

"Well, yes, sir. Let's go." She followed him inside. He closed the door behind him.

"Oh my gosh! Will you look at this! I can't believe my eyes!" Her jaw dropped as she observed a Shaman's Neck Ring, a Sun Dance Shield with eagle feathers, a Warrior's Flute, men's and women's regalia, moccasins and baskets. She knew most of these things before her were burial items.

"Where on earth did you get these lovely items, Mr. Canon?"

"Oh, I've travelled around the open lands of the American Southwest and sometimes I find things. I have land outside of Santa Fe where I finds things, too." Canon confessed.

"Mr. Canon, are these things for sale? Can I buy something to take home with me today? I'd be thrilled! That is, if I can afford it. I don't know what these things would cost me." The researcher said coyly.

"Tell me what you want, Ms. Jennings, and I'll give you a price for today only." Canon replied.

"Well, how much is that Neck Ring up there on the wall?" she pointed.

"That would be thirteen hundred dollars." The owner said.

"How about that old flute with the leather strands hanging from it?" she asked.

"I'll sell that today for one thousand dollars. Just for you, Ms. Jennings." Canon said with a smile.

"Well, sold for one thousand dollars! That's the exact amount I wanted to spend today and I have cash. Will you wrap it up for me, please, and can I get a receipt?" She handed him the cash.

"I'll have it wrapped for you, but I don't give receipts for my personal collection. This is a private deal. I can tell you it's a Cherokee Warrior's Flute and it's very old. You have something special there." They shook hands. Canon escorted her to the front of the gallery, where she waited on a wooden bench for her purchase. Canon returned to his office.

A young woman walked by and stopped to ask if she was finding everything all right. "Oh yes, yes. I just bought something from the owner's private collection and I'm so happy! Thank you for asking." The researcher smiled.

A man with a baseball cap approached with her package. "Here you are, Miss." She thanked him and left the gallery. She had to call agent Garland.

CHAPTER 14

After the morning meeting, agent-in-charge Garland checked his computer. A message from Chief Romero had an attachment. "Film-May 15 to May 17, SF parking lot." He dialed Marc.

"Can you come to my office? I want you to look at this camera footage." Garland said urgently.

Garland zoomed in on the images. He saw the yellow VW Bug. A blue sedan pulled in two spaces away. Someone got out of the sedan and stood by the VW. The person was tall and thin, with long light-colored hair. A woman. She bent down by the VW, then got up again. She looked around, men approached and got into another vehicle. She walked around the lot and came back to the VW. She had something in her hand, then knelt down again."

Marc entered. "What do you have, sir?"

"Look at this, agent. The date is May 15, Friday afternoon. It looks like a woman. I'll play back the footage." Marc saw the tall woman get out of the blue car and walk over to the VW. There was something in her hand. She bent down out of view of the camera and got up again. She walked to the other side of the VW.

Garland said "This person could be slashing the back rear tires when she bends down. Notice how she looks around before she kneels down, then looks around again before returning to her vehicle."

"This looks like it could be Anita Boles, the gallery manager. I'd like to get a better look at her face. Can you zoom in on the face?" Marc squinted for a closer look. "Yes, that's her!" He exclaimed.

"Let's verify the make and model of Anita's car. We'll need her home address. Is this enough for a warrant, sir? We have her in possession of Joyce's necklace and at the scene of Joyce's car. Anita must have slashed the tires while Joyce was at work. She'd know Joyce would need a ride home, and would return to the gallery to make a call." Marc said.

"It looks like she was involved, but we don't know who took Joyce home that night and who poisoned her. I'll get a warrant. Call Chief Romero and tell him to bring her in for questioning." Marc left and Garland got back on the phone.

Police Chief Romero was looking at his computer when

a desk Sergeant asked to speak to him. "Excuse me, sir. I just got a tip from the Santa Fe Journal saying there's going to be a protest today at four p.m. at the J.D. Canon Gallery. The reporter got word from the Pueblo Council that Elders and their attorneys will be there. They're accusing the owner of selling stolen American Indian artifacts."

"Ok, Sergeant. Thanks." Romero's phone rang. It was FBI agent Bennett.

"Chief, Anita Boles is the prime suspect in Joyce Jordan's murder. We'd like you to bring her in for questioning." Marc explained.

"What do you have so far, agent?" The Police Chief asked.

"The necklace found in Anita's drawer had Joyce's prints on it and the family said it was hers. She always wore it. After looking closely at camera footage you sent, it's the suspect in the parking lot by Joyce's car. Maybe Boles or someone else from the gallery drove Joyce home." Marc said.

"Ok, I'll send some officers to pick her up. And agent, we just got a tip that Pueblo Elders will be staging a protest at the gallery today at four p.m. Can you come up here? We could use more help around here today." The Chief said.

"Yes, I'll come up with more agents. We sent a researcher undercover to the gallery, Chief. She'd recognize burial items if she saw them. We're waiting to hear back from her anytime now." Marc hung up.

Marc decided to call Laura on her new cell phone. She

had seen Anita's car. Laura was on her lunch break sitting along the Alameda. "Hi Marc, what's new?"

"Laura, remember you said Anita wanted to give you a ride the other day? What color was her car? Can you describe it?" Marc asked urgently.

"It was blue. It was a sedan, with four doors, I think. Why?" Laura asked.

"Be careful, Laura. Anita is our prime suspect in Joyce's murder." Marc cautioned.

"Laura, we believe Anita slashed Joyce's tires. The police will be picking her up for questioning. Keep your distance." Marc said and hung up.

Maureen got back to her car and drove a few blocks away from the gallery. She parked the car and took off the wig, then dialed the FBI office. "Agent Garland, J.D. Canon just sold me a flute. It would have been buried with the warrior who owned it. I got a good look at his collection. Much of what I saw must have been stolen by him or someone else. I paid cash and he wouldn't give me a receipt. He said it was a private deal."

"Good work, Ms. Jansen. Can you stand by? I'm getting a warrant to search the gallery premises. I'm sending a team of agents and a truck to retrieve the stolen items and human remains. I'll need you to help with the inventory." Garland explained.

"Sure, I'll be here. I'll get some lunch and buy a change

of clothes. I'll need gloves to handle the items, too." Maureen hung up and drove to the Plaza. She'd eat at the cafe by the Palace of the Governors. Then, go to the camping store down the street for some casual clothes and gloves. Things were going to get messy.

After speaking to the researcher, agent Garland called the Santa Fe Police Chief Romero. "Chief, the undercover researcher just bought a stolen burial item from J.D. Canon today. She said his collection is filled with stolen Indigenous artifacts. That's enough for a search warrant of the premises. I'm sending Marc Bennett and a team of agents to the gallery now."

"Ok, agent. I sent officers to pick up Anita Boles. I'll keep her here for questioning. I got a warrant to search her car and home." The Chief replied.

"Marc's gallery informant said Anita's car is a blue sedan. The same car we saw in the camera footage you sent. It should be on the gallery premises." Garland added.

"It looks like all hell is going to break loose at the J.D. Canon Gallery today." The Chief said, then hung up the phone.

CHAPTER 15

Laura returned to the gallery after eating lunch on the Alameda. She saw Anita as she entered.

"Laura, there you are. I need to speak to you for a minute." She waved for Laura to come to her office.

Laura approached hesitantly. She remembered she had some pepper spray in her purse. She opened the purse and tucked the spray in her pocket. "What's on your mind, Anita?" Laura asked.

"Laura, I'm missing something from my office and wondered if you knew anything about it. You were here a few days ago while I went to get the artwork for your customer. Remember?"

"Yes, while I was waiting for you and Gianni, my customer,

I stayed here admiring the artwork. What are you missing?" Laura asked innocently.

"There was something in my drawer that's no longer there. It was something very personal. I think you took it." Anita accused.

"Anita, other people come through your office every day. Why are you accusing me?" Laura asked.

"Stop playing the innocent schoolteacher, you little sneak! I see the way Mr. Canon dotes on you. You're trying to break up his marriage, aren't you?" Anita had a wild look in her eyes now.

Laura dipped her hand into her pocket and said. "No, Ms. Boles, I didn't steal anything and I resent your accusations! I'm going back to my station now." She head toward the door.

Anita stood up from behind her desk and closed the door before Laura could leave. "I could have you fired for this! I heard you asking questions about Joyce, too. I told you not to discuss her! You're not following my rules, Laura." The taller woman held a pen, raised her fist and was ready to strike Laura's face.

Laura took out the pepper spray and aimed it at the manager's face. "Get out of my way!" Laura sprayed the pepper and Anita bent over coughing and holding her eyes. Laura ran out of the office door.

J.D. Canon came out of his office and Laura ran past him. "What's going on out here?" he demanded.

"She tried to attack me." Laura said panting. Some of the pepper hit her, too.

Just then, the entry door opened and two officers walked in. They noticed the woman standing near the owner was in distress.

"Hello, officers. What can I help you with?" asked the owner.

"We're looking for Anita Boles."

Laura approached them. "Oh, officers. I'm so glad you're here! She's making false accusations and just tried to attack me, so I sprayed her with paper spray. She's vicious!" Laura said with shortness of breath.

The officers found Anita coughing. "Ms. Boles, we're taking you into custody for the murder of Joyce Jordan. You have the right to remain silent. You have the right to an attorney. Anything you say can and will be used against you in a court of law."

"Officers, you must be mistaken! I've known Anita for years. She wouldn't kill anyone." J.D. looked at his loyal manager in disbelief. "Anita, you said you fired Joyce. That's all. I'm sure there's just been a misunderstanding."

Anita looked up at her boss. Her face was blotchy from the pepper. Her eyes were red and hair tangled. "Whatever I do, I do for you, Mr. Canon." She was hand-cuffed and led away to a squad car by the front entrance.

Laura went to straighten up before returning to her

station. On her way back, she looked for Carol. She found her alone in the Textile Room. There were no visitors.

"Carol, Anita tried to attack me! Then, police arrived and took her in as a suspect in Joyce's death. I'm still shaking!"

Carol put her arm around the young woman to calm her. "Did she know you took the necklace?" Carol asked.

"She suspected I took something personal and I denied it. Carol, I gave the necklace to the FBI and they found Joyce's prints. It was hers. The FBI agent told me today he thinks Anita slashed Joyce's tires. He told me to be careful." Laura stopped to take a deep breath.

"Laura, let's stay calm and take care of the visitors. The Canons must be distraught knowing their friend and manager is in police custody. Personally, I'm glad she's gone. I'll work the front rooms. You work the others. We'll act normal until we're told the gallery is closed or until something else happens." Carol said with authority.

"Carol, another thing. Anita said I was trying to break up Mr. Canon's marriage. I would never do that! He told me he wants me to stay on past summer, that I should quit teaching because I've made big sales for the gallery. I was tempted." Laura explained.

"I told you the owner has an eye for young women. Anita is protective of him and his family, so gets suspicious of any little thing. I'm sure you wouldn't be so brazen as to try to break up his marriage. You don't seem the type. Also, Anita would never let you stay on full-time, no matter what Canon told you. Let's get to work, Laura. There are still visitors in the gallery."

CHAPTER 16

Meanwhile, Marc Bennett was driving on the Interstate with fellow agents in black vehicles and a black unmarked truck. All were headed north to Santa Fe. They had their orders to search the gallery premises for stolen burial items. Agent Bennett had a search warrant. It was nearly two p.m. when they arrived in the parking lot across from the J.D. Canon Gallery. Marc called Chief Romero to say he was here.

"OK, agent Bennett. I'm glad you're here. I have Anita Boles in custody. We have a warrant to search her car, office and home. Two officers are searching her car as we speak. Two are at her home. I'll get to the gallery with another officer." The Chief said.

Marc directed the group. "Agent Williams, drive the truck

around to the back entrance. You'll need to unload the tables and a ladder to take to the owner's office. Agents Janelle and Roybal, park near the truck. You'll search the residence. Keep the family separated from J.D. Canon. Wear your vests, take cuffs and keep your radios on." The agents drove off with their instructions.

"Agents Martinez and Yazzie, come with me. You'll assist with the identification and inventory. One more thing. There will be a protest here in about two hours. The Santa Fe police will assist in crowd control so, hopefully, we can proceed with our search. Let's go."

Agent Bennett put on his FBI vest and gathered his gear. The three agents crossed the busy street and approached the gallery entrance. There was a local squad car parked next to a blue sedan in the far corner. Officers were searching the vehicle.

Garland had called Maureen Jansen to go back to the gallery, so she was waiting there. She had gloves in her pocket, a camera around her neck and was carrying a wrapped package.

"Hello, Ms. Jansen. What do you have there?" Marc asked.

"This is the flute Mr. Canon sold to me. It's a burial item and proof he's selling them. I'll return it to the inventory list we compile and photograph it with the other items we retrieve today." Maureen replied.

The FBI agents and the researcher entered the gallery.

Carol was there now, since Anita was gone. "Hello agents. What can I help you with?"

Marc showed his badge. "Hello Carol. I was here the other day. You may remember me. We're here to see Mr. Canon. Please escort visitors out of the gallery. It will be closing early today."

The agents proceeded to the owner's office where they found J.D. Canon behind his desk. Marc and Maureen entered first.

"Mr. Canon, the FBI and the local police have a warrant to search your gallery for stolen Indigenous items. Unless you have papers to authenticate your collection, we will confiscate these items and place you under arrest." Marc explained.

The owner rose from his chair and said "Why this is preposterous! You have no right to accuse me of stealing. I've been in business here for years! This is my personal collection. I don't sell anything. You have no proof!"

Maureen approached him and unwrapped her package. "Why, hello there Mr. Canon. Remember me, Ms. Jennings from New Orleans?" She said in a southern drawl. "I was just here this morning and you sold me this lovely flute for one thousand dollars cash, no receipt. You said you didn't give receipts for sales from your private collection."

Canon's jaw dropped. "Ms. Jennings."

"Well, no, I'm actually Maureen Jansen, a researcher with OAS. I'm working with the FBI to identify burial items. Like those you have here." Maureen waved her arm towards the walls.

Marc called in American Indian agents, Yazzie and Martinez. They scanned the room and shook their heads in disbelief. They proceeded to set up fold-out tables around the room. They brought in a ladder to retrieve items hanging from the ceiling.

Agent Yazzie glared at the gallery owner and said. "Mr. Canon, I see sacred items here. You'll need to show proof of where you got these."

Canon began to search his desk and file cabinets. "What about my family?"

"We have agents in the residence right now. Your family is being questioned. Agents will search there, as well. If you don't have receipts of origin, the researcher, along with Mr. Yazzie, from the Navajo Nation and Ms. Martinez, from Cochiti Pueblo here will be identifying the burial items. Those items will be photographed and inventoried. They will go with us to be returned to the Tribal Nations." Marc stated.

Marc left the office and proceeded to the shipping department, where Tom was packing something.

"FBI. Stop right there!" Marc yelled. The man in the cap stopped what he was doing and put his hands up.

"OK, OK, what's going on?" Tom asked.

"The owner is accused of selling stolen burial items across state lines. The gallery is being searched as we speak. What are you packing?" Marc approached and looked in the box. There were two masks in bubble wrap. "Where's the invoice for this?"

"We don't send invoices for certain items. It's a private deal between Mr. Canon and the buyer. There is no paperwork." Tom said.

Tom realized he may be arrested. He decided to make a run for it. He pretended to look for some papers, but instead, took out a switchblade. When the agent turned to look around the room, Tom held up the knife and lunged at Bennett. He hit just above the vest. Marc felt a sharp pain in his shoulder, then turned and knocked the knife out of Tom's hand. Tom tried to run out the back door and Marc grabbed him. They wrestled and Marc spun the man down to the floor, face down. He pulled out his handcuffs and put them on Tom's wrists.

"You're under arrest for assaulting an officer of the law and possible co-conspiracy to sell stolen items. This place is loaded with federal agents. What were you thinking, Tom?" Marc asked while wincing in pain.

"I didn't know the place was being searched, so I wanted to run. I work for J.D. Canon. I do what he tells me. That's all." Tom explained.

"Did you have something to do with Joyce Jordan's murder? Is that the knife used to slash her tires?" Marc demanded.

"I don't know. I didn't do it. Anita asked to borrow my knife a few weeks ago. She didn't say why. She gave it back right away, so I didn't ask questions." Tom said as he was panting.

Marc read Tom his rights. "You have the right to remain silent. Anything you say can and will be used against you in a court of law. You have the right to an attorney."

Marc brought Tom out to the front office and cuffed him to a bench. Just then, Chief Romero and another officer entered the gallery.

"Agent Bennett. Who do you have here?" The Chief asked.

"Tom, here, works in shipping. He just assaulted me with a knife. It's probably the same knife used to slash Joyce's tires. He said Anita Boles borrowed it. It's on the floor in the shipping area. Check it for prints. Canon's in his office. Agents are taking inventory. The premises are being searched." Marc summed up the activity. "What about Boles? Did your officers find anything?"

"They searched her car and found a brown vial of white powder in her console. It's in the toxicology lab now. They, also, found a barrette under the passenger seat. White, with red diamonds, beaded. It's being checked for prints. It may be the victim's. Boles asked for an attorney. The only thing she's said is that whatever she did, she did for J.D. Canon." The Chief replied.

"I'm going to go check on my shoulder. The blade hit me." Marc looked for the restroom. He found the staff lounge first. He saw Laura and Carol sitting there.

Laura stood up and approached him. "Marc! I'm so glad to see you!" She looked at his pained face and asked "What's wrong?"

"I need some gauze and sterile solution. Do you have a first aid kit here?" he asked.

Carol replied. "Yes, right here." She opened the cabinet door and found a white box on the top shelf. She put it on the table and opened it.

Laura asked. "What happened, Marc?"

He sat down and slowly took off his protective vest. "I got stabbed by Tom. He's under arrest. I need to clean the wound."

The women helped the agent take off his bloodied shirt and they inspected the wound. Carol spoke. "The cut is about two inches long, but not too deep. We'll clean it for you, but you may need stitches." While Carol cleaned the wound she said. "You're the guy who was looking at bronzes the other day." Laura opened the sterilized pads and gauze packets to assist Carol.

"Yeh, that's me. I'm Marc Bennett, FBI. I've been undercover. Laura here has been assisting me in getting information. Some important information was relayed from you, Carol." Marc said.

"Oh, what do you mean?" Carol asked as she applied antibiotic ointment.

"You told Laura that you saw Anita wearing a copper necklace that was similar to what Joyce wore. That was a good lead. Laura found the necklace and we got Joyce's prints. Her family confirmed it was the one they gave her. Thank you."

"I liked Joyce. She didn't deserve to die like that. I didn't tell the police I saw the necklace when I was questioned because Anita was hovering over me. I should have spoken up sooner." Carol apologized.

"The Chief said they found a white powder in Anita's car. It's being tested for poison. The knife that Tom stabbed me with today was lent to Anita a few weeks ago. She didn't say why. It's being checked for prints. Anita is being held as the lead suspect in Joyce's murder." Marc said as he buttoned his shirt and painfully put on his vest.

"Thanks for your help, ladies. An agent will be interviewing you soon. In about an hour, there's going to be a protest in front of the gallery. The visitors are gone and the gallery is closed. Stay here for now. We may need your help once the protest starts."

Marc went back to Canon's office. The tables were getting filled with masks, shields, eagle feathers, regalia and more. Maureen was taking photographs and writing down descriptions of the numbered items.

Chief Romero was standing by Canon. "J.D., I want

you to know that your manager has been charged with the murder of Joyce Two Feathers Jordan and the shipper, Tom, has been charged with assaulting an officer and conspiracy to ship stolen items out of state. Your gallery and home are being searched."

Canon had been quiet as he searched for paperwork. He searched receipts for the Navajo Yei Masks and the Medicine Bundles, but he couldn't find any. Nor did he have receipts for the Apache buckskin girl dress or wooden headdress worn in the important puberty ceremonies.

He did find receipts for some of the men's beaded and quilled buckskin shirts he had bought over the years. These shirts were often portrayed in western paintings, so artists bought them. There were receipts for some of the beaded moccasins, as well. No receipts for the Sun Dance Shields and Shaman's Neck Rings. No receipts for the Cherokee War Flutes or burial baskets.

Canon showed Chief Romero receipts for some of his collection. They weren't enough to keep him from being arrested.

"J.D. Canon, you have the right to remain silent. You have the right to an attorney. Anything you say can and will be used against you in a court of law." The gallery owner was hand-cuffed.

CHAPTER 17

Marc's cell phone rang as he roamed the gallery premises. "Marc, Marshal Ross here."

"Hey, Martin. Where are you?"

"I'm in Santa Fe. I went to Joyce's dorm room with campus security and retrieved some possessions for her family. Do you have an update for me?" Ross asked.

"Yes. We have Anita Boles in custody at the Santa Fe Police Department. Police found a vial of cyanide in her car. The same car we saw in the camera footage at the parking lot. They found a barrette under the seat with Joyce's prints on it. Anita used another staffer's switchblade to slash the tires. Her prints are on the knife. "Marc explained.

"Good. It sounds like you've got Joyce's killer." Ross said.

"I'm at the gallery now. We're searching the premises.

Also, a protest is set to start in a few minutes. Park in the lot across from the gallery." Marc said.

"I'll see you soon, agent." Ross replied.

Marc went to the owner's office. Maureen Jansen and the two agents had collected most items from the office, excluding two buckskin shirts that were newer and had receipts for purchase. "We're about done here. We need to go to the residence and see what is there to inventory and take back." Maureen said.

"Ok, see what you can find." Marc told them. "You'll have to check the shipping department, too."

Chief Romero stood by the owner, who was now in hand-cuffs. His radio announced. "Chief, there are pick-up trucks and cars circling the parking lot across from the gallery. Men wearing bright-colored bandanas around their foreheads are sitting in the backs of pick-up trucks. They're yelling and raising their fists." The Chief heard cars honking in the background.

"Ok, the protest is beginning. Keep them away from the crime scene tape and the squad car. Direct them to gather by the front entrance. Keep it calm, officer."

The officer stood by the front entrance as the Tribal Nations' Elders and their attorneys gathered, along with singers and the Press. Chairs were set up in a circle around a large drum. More chairs were set up around the circle of singers where the Elders sat. The drumsticks pounded in rhythm.

Soon, the singing started. The Elders had tall poles with red cloths tied around the tops. They raised their poles up and down to the beat of the drum. Behind them, stood men and women in suits, their attorneys. Roaming around the group were reporters and camera crew.

Marc Bennett went to the front entrance and saw the large group of protesters. The scene looked ominous. The Elders were staring at the officer by the door.

Soon, the drumming stopped and someone spoke in a bull horn. "J.D. Canon, you have our sacred burial items. We demand you return them to us now!"

The drumming resumed at a faster tempo and singers were louder. The sound was deafening!

Marc returned to find Chief Romero in the gallery on his radio. He was calling available officers on the premises to come to the front.

"Chief, we have to address the protesters outside. The Elders want a response to their demands." Marc said in urgence.

"Yes, I know. We can start by telling them the truth. We have Canon under arrest for looting burial items. We have specialists going through the collection right now." The Chief said.

"Ok, let's do it, Chief." They opened the gallery door to

a crowd of angry faces and the loud beating of the drum. Chief Romero came out first, then agent Bennett and two other police officers. The Chief motioned for the drumming to stop. They stood together with television cameras focused on them. They introduced themselves to the crowd.

The Chief began. "We understand why you are here today and want to give you some important information. I am Santa Fe Police Chief Romero and this is agent Bennett with the FBI. There are other officers assisting us today." He looked at agent Bennett and nodded for him to address the group.

"The FBI was informed recently that sacred items may have been looted from Indigenous graves around the Southwest and were in a private collection at this gallery, and possibly in other private collections around the country." He was interrupted by people yelling "Grave robber! Grave robber!" and more drumming.

The Chief motioned for the crowd to quiet down and spoke. "With the undercover efforts of the FBI, we discovered that was, in fact, the case here. We have arrested the owner, J.D. Canon, for looting of burial items and selling across state lines." The crowd erupted in cheers. The Elders held their posts high in the air.

The Chief again motioned for the crowd to quiet down and listen.

Marc explained. "Right now, we have two American

Indian FBI agents and a researcher from OAS looking at the items in question. They are making an inventory of everything they find on the premises that are identified as burial items that have no receipts of purchase."

An Elder called out. "Where are you taking these items?"

"They will be carefully packed and transported to a secure location in Albuquerque. The FBI will hold them until they are reclaimed by the Tribal Leaders and families." Marc said loudly. His voice was getting raspy and his shoulder was aching from the wound.

Another Elder spoke. "I came from the Navajo Nation many miles from here. I want to see these items now." He insisted. People began to chant "Now! Now! Now!" The drumming started again.

The Chief waved to the crowd to silence. "This is an active crime scene. Agents are working through-out the premises. We will discuss this matter and come back." Drumming resumed, quieter now, as the Chief and agent Bennett went back into the gallery.

"What do you want to do, Chief?" asked agent Bennett.

The Chief thought a moment and said. "Let's escort J.D. Canon out in hand-cuffs to show them we're serious. Then, we can have small groups of four or five come in to view the collection. Give the attorneys your card. Tell them to contact you to schedule picking up their items at a later date. Write their names on the inventory list next to items they claim.

Let's have Agents Yazzie and Martinez assist them in the office."

"It sounds like a plan. I'll go out front with the other officers and make way for you to bring out Mr. Canon." Marc said before he went back outside.

"I need to call my attorney." Canon pleaded.

"You can call from the Police Station." The Chief replied.

The officers edged the crowd away from the parked squad car. The gallery door opened and out came J.D. Canon. Cameras focused on him now. The crowd jeered and yelled. "Grave robber! Looter!" The drumming got loud again. "Grave robber! Thief!" The Chief stood next to the gallery owner as the officers kept the crowd at bay. Canon's head hung low as he approached the squad car. He was leaving his beloved gallery.

After seeing Canon led away, the Elders took out sage sticks and lit them. One by one, they waved the smoke around their faces and body for spiritual cleansing.

The smudge sticks were passed around for others to purify their spirits.

CHAPTER 18

The camera crews left after getting statements from Tribal attorneys.

Marc spoke to the crowd. "We will have one group enter at a time, starting with the Navajo Nation. Next will be the Apache Nation and then the Pueblos. An officer inside will escort you to the viewing area. If you identify something, give the agent your name to be added to the Inventory List. I will give the attorneys my card. You can contact me to schedule a date for the return of your items. Please leave the premises when you are finished viewing."

Marc went inside with the first group. He watched them as they entered the office. After scanning tables carefully, they identified Yei Masks, Medicine Bundles, and two Shaman's Neck Rings. The men were somber as they left.

The Apache Nation Elders came next. They identified Warrior Shields, women's regalia and fans of eagle feathers as theirs.

The Pueblo Nations came in and Elders identified burial pottery, beaded moccasins, an Elder's staff, a rabbit skinned cloak and two Warrior Shields.

A group approached agent Bennett. One man spoke. "Agent Bennett, I am Professor John Buffalo from UNM. I am here with Elders Mirabal and Reese from the Pueblo Council. We came to this gallery some days ago and saw this collection. We knew many of these items were stolen. We organized the protest."

"I read about you in the Albuquerque Times. I presume you gave the FBI the anonymous tip." Marc recounted.

"Yes, I will admit I did. We want to thank you for following through on this important work. Some might have disregarded it." The professor held out his hand.

Marc shook his hand and said "Professor Buffalo, your initial actions were crucial to what we did here today. Be assured, the FBI will return your burial items." The Elders nodded their heads in agreement.

They were the last group to leave the gallery.

Marc went to the staff lounge where he found Carol and Laura. He looked for coffee and sat down. "Ladies, J.D. Canon has been arrested for looting graves and selling across state lines. Anita Boles has been arrested for the murder of

Joyce Two Feathers Jordan. The stolen items will go to an FBI location until they can be given back to the Tribal Nations. I'm waiting for U.S. Marshal Ross to arrive from the Cherokee Nation."

"Well, the gallery is closed, so we don't have a job." Carol said. "At least Joyce will have justice and the Tribal Nations will get some satisfaction."

"Marc, thanks for your hard work here." Laura said.

"It's my job." Marc replied. "You ladies can leave now. We'll finish up here and lock up. I'll make sure you get your paychecks."

The women gathered their belongings and clocked out. They exited the front door and walked around to the back where they saw a black truck being loaded with tables, a ladder and large boxes.

They stood still in the driveway in disbelief. Carol spoke first. "I've worked here five years and have many memories. There were elegant gallery receptions and famous people passed through here. I suspected some things weren't quite above board, but didn't know what to do. This place had a good reputation."

"Oh, Carol." They walked away slowly. "Do you want to get dinner? I don't want to go home yet."

"Yes, let's do that. I don't want to be alone right now." Carol replied. They walked to a nearby cafe on Canyon Road.

"What do you think you'll do now, Carol?"

"Well, I've always wanted to work at the Fine Arts Museum. After the news settles down, I'll apply for a job there. I hope they'll hire me." Carol responded.

"Oh, I think that would be great! You're so experienced and professional. I'm sure they'd want you on staff." Laura said as the waiter approached.

Laura ordered a green chile burger and beer. Carol ordered a Caesar Salad and red wine. "Carol, can I give you my phone number? I'd like to keep in touch."

"Of course! We've gone through a lot together, Laura."

CHAPTER 19

arc heard the gallery door open and in walked Marshal Ross. Marc greeted him. "It's good to see you, Martin. I wish it was under different circumstances." They shook hands.

"Osiyo. It's good to see you, too." The Marshal looked around. "So, this is the famous J.D. Canon Gallery. Joyce told her parents she was so glad to work here. What a shame. So, where is this infamous collection?"

Marc escorted him to the office and introduced him. "Agents, this is U.S. Marshal Ross from the Cherokee Nation in Oklahoma. He's going to identify some items and is assisting in the investigation."

The Marshal noticed the wooden flutes first. "This is a Cherokee Warrior's Flute. It has six holes and leather strands.

The wood is very old. It would have been buried with the warrior who used it." He examined the other three flutes. They were similar burial items.

Marc said. "Mr. Canon sold this Warrior's Flute to our undercover researcher for one thousand dollars. That's how we knew for certain that he was selling these items."

Marshal Ross moved over to the baskets. "These three smaller baskets are Cherokee burial baskets." He looked closely at one of the baskets. "There's still dirt in the reeds." Ross gave the agents his contact information for returning the items.

"Joyce noticed these and drew them in her sketchbook. She knew they were stolen. She must have said something to the owner or to someone else at the gallery. That's what got her killed." Ross stated.

Marc escorted Martin to the front of the gallery. "Martin, while you're here, I think we should question Anita Boles. See if we can get any information about her motive."

"Yes, I'd like to see her while I'm in town." The Marshal replied.

"First, I have to touch base with the other agents here. Then, I need to stop at the ER. I have a knife wound that may need stitches. While I'm there, maybe you can visit the hospital cafeteria and get dinner."

Before leaving the gallery, Marc Bennett checked in

with the other agents working on the premises. "Remove the human remains found in the den and all burial items off the premises, then lock up the gallery. I'll see you back in Albuquerque."

Marc told his passengers to ride back with the other agents, since he would remain in Santa Fe awhile.

He called agent in charge Garland to say the items would be arriving soon and to direct agent Williams to the secret location for storage.

Agent Bennett and Marshal Ross left the gallery and went to the parking lot across the street. "I'll be in my black Jeep, so you can follow me. We're going to Old Santa Fe Trail. Veer to the right as it turns into Old Pecos Trail. We'll turn right onto St. Michael's Drive then to the hospital. Let's meet in the entrance." Marc explained.

The U.S. Marshal got into his green SUV with the Cherokee Nation emblem on the side.

It was six p.m. and traffic was heavy on this two-lane road. It took twenty minutes just to drive a few miles. As he sat in traffic, Marc imagined what it was like in the early years of Santa Fe, when wagon trains came down this road bringing trading goods to the Plaza. Now, it's a main thoroughfare into a city known as one of the major art centers in the country.

Marc found a protein bar in his console and realized he hadn't eaten since seven that morning. He was feeling light-headed from the intensity of the day and from the pain in his shoulder. He needed something more to eat after he got treated in the ER.

The men parked their vehicles and went to the hospital lobby. "Marc, do you want me to go to the ER with you?"

"No thanks, it's not necessary. I hope it won't take too long. I'll meet you in the cafeteria." The men parted.

Marc proceeded to the ER and showed his badge. He was escorted to a room where he was met by the Attending Physician and a nurse. They helped him take off his shirt and inspected the wound. "Well, someone took good care of you, Mr. Bennett. The wound doesn't look infected but you will need stitches."

"Ok, Doc. Can you give me a topical pain killer? I'm still on duty and have work to do tonight. I have a long drive to Albuquerque, too." Marc said.

"Yes, we'll do that, but I wouldn't suggest you drive tonight with that pain in your shoulder. The road down La Bajada Hill can be treacherous at night."

"I'll keep that in-mind." Marc replied as he felt the sting of the needle.

In forty minutes, Marc was stitched up and discharged from the ER. He went to the cafeteria and got a green chile cheeseburger and fries. He saw Marshal Ross at a table in the back of the room.

"Are you all right, Marc?" asked Ross.

"Yes, it took ten stitches. The ladies at the gallery cleaned it and put some ointment on it earlier today. The Doc said that kept it from getting infected. I guess I'm lucky for that." Marc replied as he savored the burger.

After finishing his meal, Marc said "Martin, we have a lot of evidence on Anita Boles. I hope this will bring some closure to her family and the Cherokee Nation."

"It's good to catch a killer and I hope the charges stick. Joyce was an artist and a nice person. Everyone who knew her said the same thing. Her roommate said she was a keen observer. Being observant is how she noticed those burial items, too. Her family is taking it hard. It can be a tough world out there for young women."

"Marc, when the trial is over, I'd like to get Joyce's necklace, barrette and sketchbook back to her family. Can you follow up on that?"

"Yes, of course. I'll keep you informed as the case proceeds." Marc replied.

They walked to the parking lot. There was a colorful sunset in the making. The Sangre de Cristo mountains were now purple and streaks of orange and pink were in the west. The two men paused to feast their eyes as they looked around the landscape.

Marc said "It sure is beautiful. It's good to be outside again."

"Yes, the earth and sky replenish our spirit." Ross took

in a deep breath and held his hands up in gratitude for the beauty before him.

The men got into their vehicles and drove to the Santa Fe Police Department.

CHAPTER 20

When they arrived, they asked to see Chief Romero. The Chief was in his office. Marc introduced the men. "Chief, this is U.S. Marshal Martin Ross from the Cherokee Nation." The men shook hands.

"Good to meet you, Chief. We spoke over the phone about Joyce Two Feathers Jordan." Ross said.

"Yes, we did. Thanks for coming to Santa Fe, Marshal."

Marc spoke. "Chief, we wanted to talk to the suspect while the Marshal is here."

"Anita has an attorney and has been read her Miranda Rights. You can try, but no promises. Let's see." The Chief led them to an Interrogation Room. The suspect was brought in. The Chief stayed in the hall and listened from behind the two-way mirror.

"Hello Anita. I'm agent Bennett with the FBI and this is U.S. Marshal Ross from the Cherokee Nation."

She stared at Bennett. "You came to the gallery, didn't you?"

"Yes, I did. I came as a visitor, then undercover. The victim, Joyce Jordan, was last seen by you before her body was discovered two days later. Do you want to comment?" Marc asked.

"You were sneaking around the gallery asking questions, pretending to be a buyer. You were talking to Carol and Laura, weren't you? I told them not to talk about Joyce. They didn't follow the rules. They should be fired." Anita said coldly.

"Did Joyce follow the rules, Anita?" asked Marshal Ross.

"She did OK at first. Then she started asking questions about Mr. Canon's private collection. That wasn't any of her business. He doesn't want anyone asking questions about his collection." Anita said.

"Were you aware that Mr. Canon had stolen burial items in his collection? That's what Joyce was concerned about. Canon was looting Indigenous graves and selling items for profit." Ross stated.

"That's not my business. I don't ask him questions. I just do what I'm told. No one is supposed to ask him questions. My job was to protect Mr. Canon and his family and to sell art. Anything or anyone who got in the way had to go." She explained.

"Is that why Joyce had to go, Anita?" Marc asked.

"Yes, she had to go!" Anita said emphatically.

"You told police you fired her. That's why she didn't return to work. You said she didn't meet her sales quota. Was she fired?" Ross pushed.

"I got rid of her. That's all. I got rid of her." Anita said and crossed her arms.

"Did you slash her tires? Did you slash her tires so she would need a ride home? Did you drive her home? We have a knife with your prints on it. We found a vial of cyanide in your car. The same poison that killed Joyce. We have Joyce's necklace with your prints on it." Bennett explained.

Anita sat up. "Where did you get the necklace? I hid that in my drawer and it went missing. Was it that little sneak, Laura? I knew it! She acts so innocent, but she stole that necklace." Anita was mad.

"You took that necklace from Joyce when you killed her. You took it as a souvenir and you wore it to work after she died. Someone saw you wearing it and knew it was Joyce's. That wasn't very clever of you, Anita." Bennett said.

The suspect glared at agent Bennett. "You don't have anything on me. I'll be out of here in no time and back to work at the gallery."

Marshal Ross asked "Do you know that J.D. Canon has been arrested? The gallery is closed, Anita. Your co-worker, Tom, was arrested, too, for assaulting agent Bennett with the same knife you used to slash Joyce's tires. You won't be going back to your job or any job. We have enough evidence to keep you in jail for a long time."

Anita stood up and pounded her fists on the table. "You're lying! You're lying! You're lying! Get out! Get out!" She yelled then laid her head on the table and cried. "You're lying. You're lying."

The two men left the room and joined Chief Romero in the hall.

"Well, she's loyal to J.D. Canon. That's for sure. Let's go visit him now."

In another room the men watched as the gallery owner was brought in with hands cuffed. He had been finger-printed and processed. His attorney was with him now. They introduced each other to the agents.

Mr. Jacobs, the attorney began. "J.D. Canon wants to make a plea deal. He knows that since he doesn't have sales records or a provenance for much of his private collection, many items will be returned to the Tribal Nations. The human remains found in his den were dug up on his private land. He thought that was legal, but now understands that it wasn't and he should have informed the state of what he found."

Chief Romero asked. "J.D. Is that your legal name?"

"My legal name is Jerry David Canon. I prefer using J.D."

"OK J.D. Tell us your plea deal."

"I will put the gallery up for sale. The artwork that I don't own can return to the consignors, the rightful owners. My family and I will move out in thirty days. We're building a house in town and it should be finished by then. I will turn in my passport." He looked at the Chief. "I don't want to go to prison. You can place me on house-arrest with an ankle monitor. I want to give my employees three weeks of severance pay. Even if two of them are in jail, they still need the money."

The attorney added. "My client has no prior arrests and is a longtime member of this community. He wants to be sure his family is not charged since they didn't know how or where he got his collection. He'd like to continue to sell his art privately. Can we work something out here?"

Agent Bennett asked to be excused to call his office. He called agent Garland.

"Sir, Canon wants to make a plea deal to avoid prison time. He agreed to sell the gallery, return the stolen burial items, move off the premises, turn in his passport and be on house-arrest. He wants to sell art privately. What's your input on this?" asked Bennett.

"For the crimes he's charged with, he could get prison time and pay a fine, a large fine. He left that part out. I suggest five years of probation with a court-appointed monitor to oversee the sale of the gallery, any private sales and his financials. He will provide detailed receipts to the monitor for private sales."

Garland continued. "He should be on house arrest and wear an ankle monitor for five years. He will report weekly to his probation officer. Travel is limited to Santa Fe County. He will inform his probation officer of any travel requested outside the county and be limited to a radius of eighty miles. He will pay a fine of three hundred thousand dollars. That should do it, agent." Garland said and hung up.

Bennett looked for a cup of coffee then returned to the meeting. He retrieved a tape recorder he had in his coat pocket, placed it on the table and turned it on.

"I have a counter-offer from the FBI." Agent Bennett proceeded to repeat what he was just told, then turned to the Police Chief. "Chief Romero, do you have something to add?"

"Mr. Canon has land outside of Santa Fe where he dug up the remains of an American Indian. There should be some type of monitoring of his actions there to assure there will be no more digging up graves and artifacts. Let's set up a camera system to monitor his activities." The Chief stated.

"What do you say, Mr. Canon? Do you agree?" Bennett asked.

The attorney and his client turned to discuss the details of this countered plea deal. J.D. told his attorney "Anything is better than going to prison. Take it."

"We accept your offer." Replied the attorney. "Can my client be released on bond? He brought his checkbook."

Chief Romero replied. "I'm going to type up this plea agreement and all parties will sign. I will need a judge's final approval. Your client may be here awhile. In the mean-time you can go to the Clerk and pay the bond."

Before leaving the room, Marshal Ross addressed Canon. "Joyce Two Feathers Jordan was a Cherokee daughter and she will be missed by many. Her family is in mourning. She drew sketches of the Cherokee burial items you had in your collection. Your manager killed her because she was asking questions. She wasn't fired. She was killed to protect you!"

"Now your manager is sitting in jail for Joyce's murder. We have a lot of evidence to charge her. She killed Joyce for you! Did you know that, Mr. Canon?" Ross asked.

"I knew Anita was loyal, but I didn't think she would kill for me. She was a friend of the family. I'm very sorry about Joyce. I was told she was fired. That's all I knew. I liked her and was very sad to hear she was gone." Canon said in a serious tone.

"Joyce was killed, Mr. Canon. Murdered!" U.S. Marshal Ross pounded his fist on the table, then stood up to leave.

Marc followed his friend out of the room. He put his hand on Martin's shoulder. "I'm glad you spoke to Canon about Joyce. He needed to hear that. A young and talented woman is dead for no reason because of him."

"It's been a long day, Marc. I need to get back to my hotel. I'm heading back to Oklahoma in the morning. Wada. Thank you in Cherokee." They shook hands and the Marshal walked into the night. He looked up at the stars and raised his arms before entering his vehicle.

Marc had to wait for the document to be drawn up so he could sign for the FBI on the plea deal reached. He decided to wait in the empty lobby and make a call.

The phone rang. "Laura, it's Marc. How are you?"

"Marc, it's good to hear from you. I'm fine and Carol's fine, though we're both out of work for the time being. I'm so glad I didn't quit my teaching job like Canon insisted." Laura said.

"Yes, that's a good thing. Another good thing is that Canon wants to give you and Carol three weeks of severance pay as part of his plea deal to stay out of prison." Marc was glad to give good news for a change.

"That's great! It will sure help us out. It will carry me until school starts and will help Carol while she looks for a new job. I'll tell her. What are you doing? Are you still in town? How's your shoulder feeling?" Laura asked.

"I'm here waiting at the Police Department. I have to sign off on a plea deal the FBI and local police made with J.D. Canon. It's getting late, so I'm getting a hotel nearby. The ER doctor told me I shouldn't drive back tonight, so I'll follow his order." Marc replied.

"Hey, since you're not working in the morning, how about if we meet for breakfast before I head back to the office? How about nine a.m. at the La Fonda Hotel restaurant? I could use a good breakfast after today." Marc asked.

"That sounds great, Marc. I'll see you then." Laura replied.

It would be another hour before Marc signed off on the plea deal that the judge approved. J.D. Canon posted bond and left with his attorney.

Agent Bennett went into Chief Romero's office before leaving. "Chief, what about Tom? The man who stabbed me."

"We're keeping him overnight. He has two charges against him and wants a court-appointed attorney. He has no prior offenses. He assaulted an officer of the law, so that's serious." The Chief replied.

"Keep him here as long as you can. If he's released on bond, I'd suggest he wear an ankle-monitor." Bennett said.

"OK, agent. I will let you know what the judge decides." Chief Romero informed him.

"I'll be in town overnight before heading back tomorrow. Doctor's orders. Call if you need me." Agent Bennett left in search of a nearby hotel on Cerrillos Road. He needed some rest.

CHAPTER 21

June 11

The next morning, Laura woke up refreshed and had her morning coffee. She took her dogs for a walk on this warm June morning in Santa Fe. All she had planned for today was to make some calls and meet Marc for breakfast.

Upon returning home, she called her parents. She hadn't updated them on the recent events. It was an hour later in the Midwest, so they'd be up.

"Laura, good morning. How are you?" her mother asked.

"I'm fine, mom. I must say it's been an eventful week out here. I'm not working at the gallery any longer. It closed down yesterday." Laura explained.

"Why? What happened? Tell me you didn't quit your teaching job, Laura."

"No, no and it's a good thing I didn't. This was a more adventurous summer job than I could have imagined. It turns out, the manager was charged with the murder of a young woman who worked there before I did." Laura started.

"What? Are you alright?" her mom asked urgently.

"I'm fine, but it turns out the owner was charged with looting American Indian burial sites and selling items across state lines. The FBI was investigating him. The young woman noticed some of his collection must have been stolen, so the manager poisoned her. I found her necklace in the manager's office and gave it to the FBI. With other evidence, it all led to the manager." Laura said.

"What on earth is going on out there? Your father won't believe it. What about the owner?" her mother asked.

"He worked out a plea deal to stay out of prison. I don't know the details. Another guy, Tom, who worked there was arrested for assaulting an officer, too. So, the gallery's closed. There is some good news, though. The stolen burial items will be returned to the Tribal Nations and I'll be getting three weeks' severance pay." Laura said.

"Laura, I'm going to fly out there tomorrow. I know your father would want to come but he's working. You've been through an ordeal. I'll take a shuttle up to Santa Fe where you can pick me up. Do you have room for me on your couch? If not, I'll stay at a hotel."

"Yes, mom, I have room. My pets and I would love to have you here. Let me know when you arrive. I've got to run now. I'm meeting someone for breakfast. See you soon!" Laura noticed the time, so she decided to drive to the Plaza.

She parked on Palace Avenue and walked to the La Fonda Hotel. Laura passed a brightly colored building with a long portal. She looked at the sign. It read IAIA Museum of Contemporary Arts. She thought of Joyce. Laura would return to the gallery after breakfast.

She got to the busy restaurant and saw Marc seated at a booth. "Hello, there. I hope I'm not late." The place was bustling with visitors.

"Hi Laura, you're fine. I already started on my coffee." Marc asked. He noticed Laura's blue eyes and long curly hair. She was dressed more casual today than when working at the gallery. She was attractive, as always.

"I've heard this place has great Huevos Rancheros. It translates to Rancher's Breakfast. Hey, how's your shoulder?"

Marc looked up from the menu. "Oh, I'm OK. It's a little sore." His eyes continued scanning the menu. "Yes, here it is, Huevos Rancheros. It looks great! Shall we order two with a side of green chile?"

"Sounds good. It's funny, we seem to order the same things. Have you noticed?"

"Yes, I guess we have similar taste." Marc smiled. The waiter approached with water and took their orders.

"So, Laura, what are you going to do now that you have a few weeks off before school starts?" Marc asked.

"Well, I just spoke to my mother before I came here and told her what happened. She got very worried and decided to fly out tomorrow. She'll stay with me in Santa Fe. My place is quaint, but we'll manage. I'd like to go sight-seeing with her and visit local restaurants." Laura said.

"I'm glad to hear that, Laura. You've been under a lot of pressure and put yourself at risk playing detective. You were good at it and helped my case, but you could have gotten hurt. Anita had it out for you after suspecting you found Joyce's necklace." Marc said.

"How do you know that, Marc? Did she tell you?"

"Yes, I went to interview her last night with Marshal Ross from the Cherokee Nation. When I told her I had Joyce's necklace, she suspected you took it. She's got a real mean streak in her. If she got out of jail, she'd probably look for you. Don't worry, she's not going anywhere. We have a lot of evidence against her, thanks to you and Carol." Marc said confidently.

Their meals came, so attention was diverted to discussing food. Marc ate voraciously.

Laura commented. "This is so good. I love the green chile on my eggs. Like I said, in New Mexico, they put chile on everything! I'm going to bring my mother back here. She may not go for all the chile, but she'd like the festive atmosphere."

Marc shook his head in agreement. He finished his meal and let out a deep sigh. "That was so good. Let's meet here again before you return to school, shall we?"

"That would be nice." Laura agreed.

"When are you heading back, Marc?" Laura asked.

"I have about an hour, before I drive back. If you want, we can stroll around the Plaza." Marc suggested.

Their waiter came to clear their plates. Marc paid the bill. "Marc, there's an IAIA Gallery on the next block. I'd like to visit."

"Let's go." He replied. They proceeded out of the hotel lobby and onto the busy street. On this June day, tourists were everywhere and stores were busy with shoppers.

They saw the colorful gallery across from the Cathedral and entered. There were works by students and Alumni of IAIA. Laura asked the staffer behind the counter. "Do you have any works by Joyce Two Feathers Jordan?" He searched his computer.

"Why, yes, we have a sculpture. I'll show you." Laura looked at Marc and they followed. "Here it is, Bird in Flight." Laura thanked the young man and she stroked the stone with a gentle hand. The tag read three thousand dollars.

"Oh, Joyce. You were so talented. I'm so sorry you're not here. I feel we would have been friends." Laura whispered as she felt the contour of the stone. Tears were forming.

Marc realized he needed to call U.S. Marshall Ross to let him know that Joyce's sculpture was here. He could then notify Joyce's family. Marc would call later.

While Laura was looking at the sculpture, Marc looked at the jewelry case. Something caught his eye and he asked to see it.

It was a copper circle on a copper chain. Inside the circle was a black star with seven points. The Cherokee Star. He purchased the necklace and put the box in his coat pocket.

He approached Laura and noticed her somber mood. "Let's go, Laura." He took her arm and led her outside. They crossed the street into Cathedral Park. He found a quiet area and they sat.

"Laura, I'm glad we went to that gallery. I'll be sure Joyce's parents are aware of her sculpture. They may want it. I know you feel bad about Joyce's death. I have something you can remember her by." He took the box out and held the necklace. "This is for you."

Laura held it and cried. "Oh, the Cherokee Star. It's lovely, Marc." She leaned against him on the bench. He held her hand. "Thank you. This means a lot to me."

"Here, let me put it on your neck." She lifted her hair. Laura felt the cool metal against her skin. She held the circle and felt the star's seven points.

"I feel Joyce's presence. This is so special. I'm going to call Carol and tell her."

"Laura, I have to get going, but I want to take you and your mother out to dinner while she's here. I want to tell her what a brave daughter she has."

They stood and hugged each other amidst the crowd of visitors. He kissed her on her forehead and said "I'll see you soon." They parted ways, only for the time being.

AUTHOR'S NOTE

Many of the street names used are in existence today. La Fonda Hotel is an historic building still in use today. The names of Zozobra co-creators are real. The yearly burning of Zozobra still occurs during Fiesta in Santa Fe. The Institute of American Indian Arts (IAIA) is an actual school on the campus of the College of Santa Fe. UNM refers to the University of New Mexico and Cochiti Pueblo refers to one of New Mexico's existing American Indian Pueblos.

Across the U.S., Indigenous ruins, graves and sacred sites have been plundered for research and for profit. This was usually done without permission from the Native communities and families from which the items were taken. Items taken included human remains, sacred items, pottery and other significant Indigenous artifacts. Buying and selling these items became a profitable business and an underground market flourished. (An Indigenous Peoples' History of the United States, R. Dunbar-Ortiz 2019).

After decades of pressure from tribal governments and

individuals, Congress passed NAGPRA in 1990. The Native American Graves Protection and Repatriation Act. This requires museums and federal agencies to return burial items and human remains to their Indigenous communities. This Act was updated in 2024 providing specific timelines to facilitate the repatriation. (Dept. of the Interior, Office of the Secretary).

New Mexico has its own laws for unmarked burials. Knowingly disturbing an unmarked burial is a fourth-degree felony, with prison time and fines. If caught with items from a historically significant site, the items are to be returned to the state. A permit is required from the state medical investigator with approval from the state archaeologist and historic preservation officer. (NM Article 6-Cultural Properties Act, Section 18-6-11.2)

ACKNOWLEDGEMENTS

I want to thank author Susan McDuffie for her words of encouragement in writing this novel. She is a creative spirit, a masterful writer, and longtime friend.

I am grateful to the staff of E.M. Tippett's Book Design for their patience and assistance in answering all my questions. Their interior formatting and cover design are just what I imagined.

ABOUT THE AUTHOR

Linda A. Morton is a former educator for Santa Fe Public Schools and a former Real Estate Broker in the Chicago area. She currently resides in northern Illinois, where she tends to her landscape of native plants and a vegetable garden. She is an avid reader of mystery novels that take place in New Mexico and Arizona.